EULALIA

First Norman Abbess

THE FIRST LADIES OF SHAFTESBURY ABBEY
VOLUME II

DEBORAH M JONES

Dedicated to all the directors, staff and volunteers who work so tirelessly for the Shaftesbury Abbey Museum and Garden Trust, which brings in thousands of visitors every year. Whether their interest is in the peace of the garden, the medieval herbs, or the well-designed museum, visitors discover the Saxon origins and history of the abbey, which was the first just for women, and which became one of the wealthiest in the land. From AD 888 until its destruction in 1539, situated on a high hilltop, it dominated the countryside all around and was of national significance and influence.
www.shaftesburyabbey.org.uk

CONTENTS

Note to the Reader and Abbey Drawings	vii
Introduction I	xv
Introduction II	xvii
Part One *The Story Begins, 1074*	1
Part Two *The Consecration of the Abbess*	63
Part Three *The Story Continues*	86
Part Four *The Story Concludes, 1086-1107*	131
The Daily Prayer Life of the Nuns	147
The letters of Anselm to Eulalia *Translated from the Latin by Gillian Knight*	150
Acknowledgments	157
About the Author	159
Also by Deborah M Jones	161

NOTE TO THE READER AND ABBEY DRAWINGS

This short novel is a work of fiction, based on historical research. There is much recorded information about the leading royal and church figures featured but very little about the nuns, other than the names of many of them.

Even about Abbess Eulalia we know only that she came from Normandy (as she features in the later mortuary role of Abbess Matilda of the Abbey of the Trinity, Caen) and initiated a massive building project at Shaftesbury, including the church of which the foundations can be seen today. She also received three letters that still exist (there could have been a more extensive correspondence between them) from Archbishop, later Saint, Anselm, and she may have been the Eulalia of a vision of the Blessed Virgin Mary as recorded at the time. *The Passion of St Edward* was written by Goscelin of Saint-Bertin in Eulalia's time, presumably commissioned by her.

Of her predecessor, the Saxon Abbess Leveva, we know nothing, although we do have a record that the town of Shaftesbury was extensively destroyed by Norman soldiers between the time of the Conquest and the arrival of Eulalia. *The Domesday Book* is the key source of information about that, and of the immense wealth and importance of the women's Abbey at Shaftesbury.

If the Abbess Eulalia's life ever had been recorded, such a document would not have survived either the destruction of written material by or about women by the Protestant Reformers* or the effective destruction of Old Wardour Castle (where the archives had been taken) by the Roundheads in the Civil War.

The two sketches over the page show some of the suggested Saxon buildings, before the Normans, within the abbey precinct and the likely plan of the abbey at Shaftesbury from the Normans. These are both by Janet Swiss.

* See Janina Ramirez, *Femina: A New History of the Middle Ages, Through the Women Written Out of It*. London: Penguin Random House, 2022.

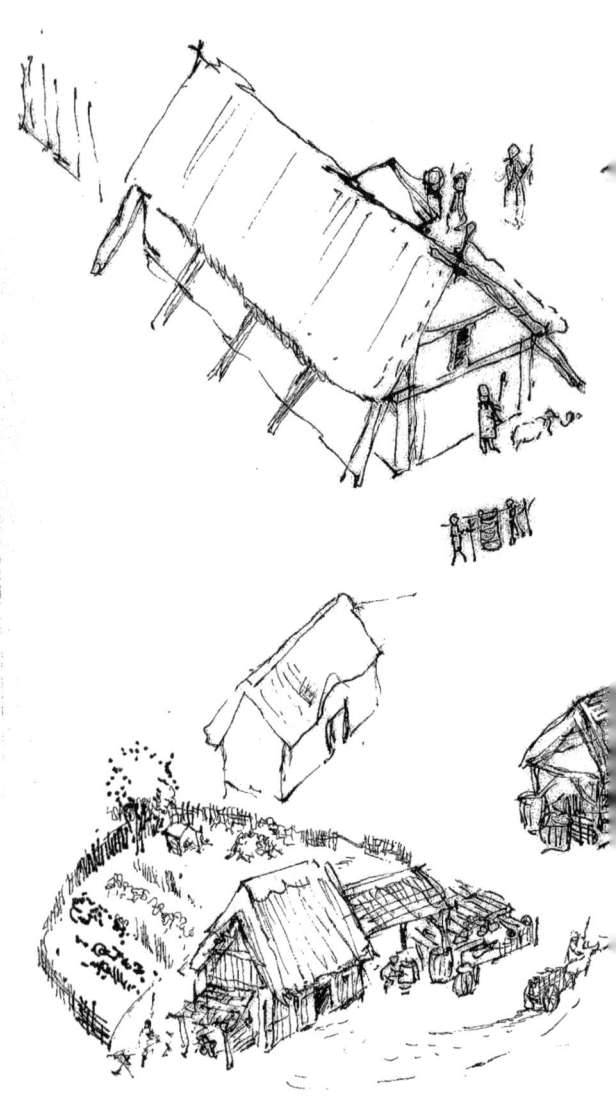

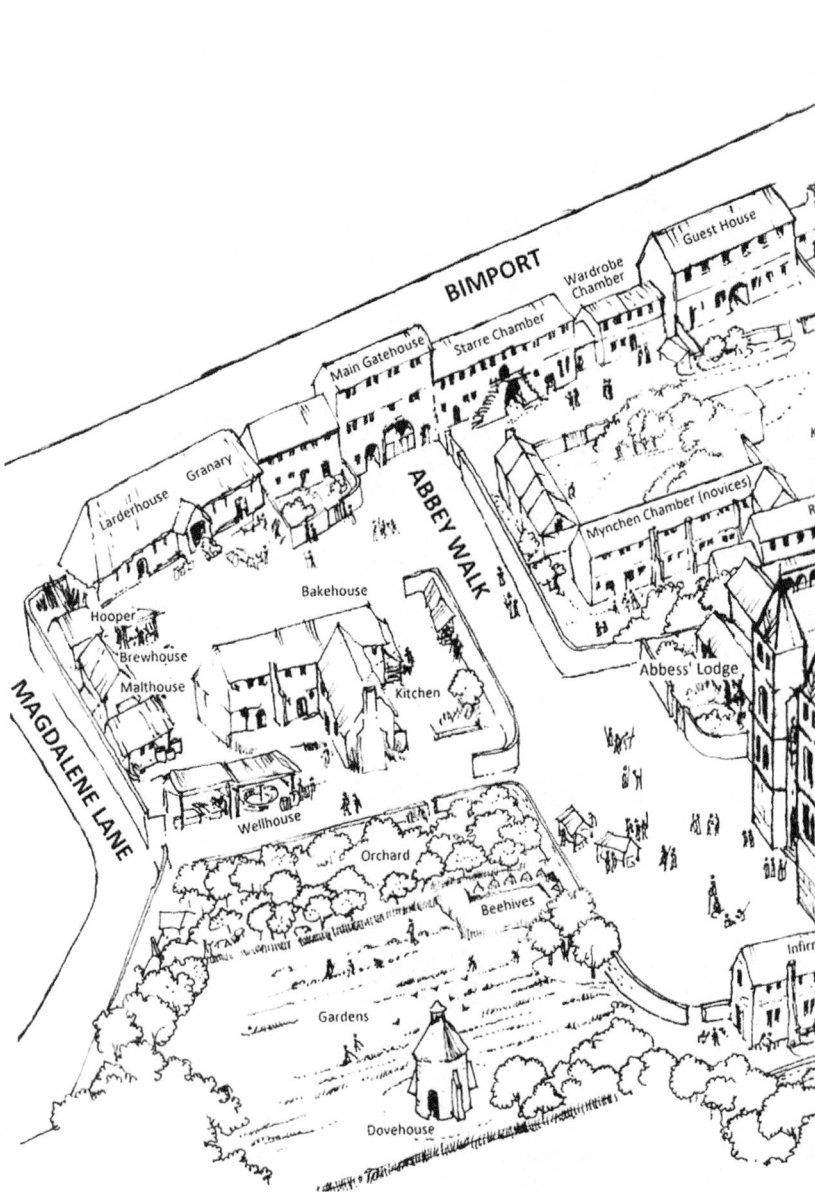

INTRODUCTION I

What this document is, and who wrote it

I, Sister Aubrey de Bosco Rohardi, archivist of this great Abbey of St Mary and St Edward, Shaftesbury, have been chosen to record a chronicle of the times of the first Norman Abbess here, Dame Eulalia, formerly of the Abbey of the Trinity, Caen. This is a great honour for which I thank God incessantly.

It is well known that King Alfred, the founder of this noble Abbey, was immortalised by the Welsh monk Asser, Bishop of Sherborne, in his Anglo-Saxon Chronicles. These are even more glorious times!

The Abbess Eulalia is very old now, tires easily and is becoming forgetful. She has been our Mother here for over thirty years, since shortly after the great Norman Conquest of the land. She feels it wise, while she can still remember details, to dictate to me a record of her rule that it may profit future generations.

This document, which you are now reading, is a work in progress and will be completed only after the death of Abbess Eulalia. So far it consists of two types of passage: the directly dictated first-person accounts, shown as "Eulalia", and the "Chronicle" passages which have already been written up into historic narrative. I have supplemented some of these latter with the memories of other people. One day, please God and when time allows, all the "Eulalia" passages will be included in the one continuous Chronicle. Until then, you will find that they alternate.

As our dear Mother is in her late sixties, it is necessary to take down as much as possible from her lips before she passes to her Eternal Reward. As she speaks, I write on parchment, and when I have transposed each section into 'Chronicle' I must then scrape and rub out the original dictation to use the skin again. So far I have used up several skins and a dozen or more quills!

I too am approaching old age, having been fifty-five years on this earth (and forty in religious life), so must work ceaselessly to capture all the memories I can and then write them up to the best of my ability. Kindly forgive any faults of memory or expression.

Benedicite omnia opera Domini!

INTRODUCTION II

The Abbess Eulalia introduces herself towards the end of her life

"Killed by nuns? We are being murdered by nuns, our Sisters in Christ. Can this be?"

These were almost my first words on arriving in Shaftesbury.

Then Sister Cecilia responded, "Well, Pope Benedict VI was murdered by one of his own priests — so such things are not unheard of. But I don't think they meant to murder us, not really. A tragic accident, no doubt."

That was so like Sister Cecilia, a learned young woman of impeccable lineage and such a calming influence and balance for me — as I am more quickly roused to emotion. She is capable, reassuring and comforting. I knew as soon as I was appointed as Abbess that she should be my Prioress *once we were established. Dear Queen Matilda of Flanders, wife of the most noble King William of Normandy and England, was so good as to raise me to this honour. In my three decades here so much has been achieved. I am expecting Archbishop Anselm of Canterbury, my good friend, to come to Shaftesbury to consecrate our glorious new church and the fine stone cloister. Of course many houses, workshops and storage buildings have been built or improved both here and throughout the extensive lands that we hold. That is far from all we have achieved. My legacy will last here for centuries to come, maybe even for ever. All for the glory of God.*

I have chosen as chronicler and scribe a woman from a most noble family. Sister Aubrey is most loyal to me and brought with her all the land and tithes of Broughton Gifford, about thirty miles away, when she entered Shaftesbury Abbey.

PART ONE
THE STORY BEGINS, 1074

Chronicle: Setting Sail

One blustery April morning in the Year of Our Lord 1074, the small fishing port of Ouistreham on the Normandy coast was presented with the unusual sight of a dozen Religious Sisters, in full Benedictine habit. Sworn to remain forever in their abbey, it would take only a momentous event to cause them to leave it, and even more to move from their native land.

They formed a tight-knit group alongside a knarr (merchant ship). Since the Glorious Conquest of 1066, some of the larger dakkars (warships) had been adapted for ferrying merchandise and civilian passengers, but the knarrs were purpose-built for trade. At the fore area, a group of three richly-clad merchants, whose complexions were darker and costumes more elaborate than those of the native Normans, were also preparing to embark, carefully stowing their wooden and leather-bound trunks beneath the soaring prow. The trade in silks and spices had begun to flourish with the new regime in Britain, so merchants were accustomed to sea voyages. Even so, they threw cautious glances from time to time at the soldiers accompanying the Sisters.

Protecting their female charges were half a dozen armed and helmeted soldiers. In high spirits the men were joshing and flirting with the nuns' three skittish young female servants. Having accompanied the party from their great convent at Caen, the warriors, now dismounted, were helping the servants to heave on board quantities of luggage from carts drawn up alongside. They had to store heavy wooden cases, containing precious books and parchment and vellum for manuscripts. As they hoisted large barrels and flagons of wine and cider they joked that they would break them open and drink the contents. This was met with raucous laughter from the maids which came to a sudden stop as the leader of the nuns froze them with a fierce glare and pursed lips. They then turned their attention to stashing on board large cloth bags bulging with linens and with hemp-canvas sacks of plate, carefully wrapped in wool, destined for church and refectory. The nuns suppressed their anxiety by praying silently for divine protection against the watery perils ahead.

Once all was stowed, crewmen secured the mound of goods with ropes running over them and, with complicated knots, tied to iron rings attached to the ship's sides.

When all was ready for the party to clamber aboard, crewmen and soldiers held the women's arms to help each of them along the plank and onto their benches just below the steeply-curved stern. The Sisters sat facing each other, under an awning designed to protect the high-status passengers from the weather and wave-spray. The servants seated themselves on more open benches and smiled and waved to the soldiers who waved back as they mounted their horses, and blew kisses to the giggling girls. This behaviour was much frowned upon by the nuns, and several tut-tuts were heard — and ignored. The biggest adventure of all their lives was about to begin.

When loaded, the muscular crew, seated on several pairs of benches midships, dipped their oars into the water, unfurled the large square red and white striped sail and set off on a course north-north-west. Under the direction of the captain, a sun-burnt veteran of many a Norman voyage of exploration and conquest, the voyage began well, the ship cutting through the water with the rhythmic action of the rowers.

However, storm clouds threatened.

The mild breeze from the south, which promised perfect sailing conditions, turned suddenly to become a violent westerly gale. The sail was taken up and the oarsmen obliged to tack into the wind as the waves became steeper. At the start, white horses crested each set of waves. Then the waves grew in size, becoming a series of watery walls falling into deep troughs, with spray showering crew and passengers alike whenever the vessel smacked against a rising wave. The curved bow had to face into the direction of the wind, and toss and plough, heart-stoppingly up and sickeningly down, or the power of wind and wave would topple the ship if they hit her broadside.

As the rowers heaved the vessel onward whenever they caught a wave, the nuns and serving-women alternately shrieked or moaned. Most of them lost their breakfast of bread and fruit, and apologised incessantly to their neighbours whose habits and clothes became soiled. The salty surges breaking over the ship's sides soaked the garments of the terrified women and swirled around their frozen feet. The fear of capsizing was very real when at length, after some collective female cries of fear, Dame Eulalia's voice rose above the din of wind and wave,

"Sisters, stop! Take heart! Cease this stupid shrieking. We must turn to God to protect us. Quiet now! Pray, pray all of you, to all the Saxon saints to whose land we travel."

The sisters went quiet, trying to recall which saints they were. The servants, leaving complex prayers to the professionals, simply repeated "Oh my God!" under their breath.

Their Abbess-elect felt gratified and a little proud of the effect the distraction had caused. She continued, in an even more commanding tone, interrupted by crashing waves:

"Let us call upon that ... sainted Queen Elfgivu, one of those holy ... bodies who lie in the very abbey to which we are travelling ... She rewards the pilgrims who visit her bones with good ... health. Will she not take especial care of us ... coming to live in her abbey all the way from Caen?'

Her throat was hoarse from shouting into the wind, so she gave up further exhortation.

To distract herself from her own fear of drowning in this treacherous water, Dame Eulalia studied the faces of the Sisters sitting opposite, seeing in each one deep anxiety. There was old Sister Anne-Marie, her grey face lined and tearful, mumbling prayers or biblical verses repetitively, while clutching her hands together tightly. Next was Sister Cecilia, possessed of intelligence and great self-control, now looking concerned, with compressed lips and deep frown-lines between her eyes, staring down in silent supplication. Her neighbour was Sister Alicia, small and sallow, whose dark eyes stayed tightly shut and whose mouth emitted low moans whenever a new wave struck. The twins, Sister Adeliza and Sister Rotza, clutched each other's hands and stared at each other for much of the voyage. Sister Suzanna, not possessed of great intelligence, looked about her with surprise at the unfamiliar surroundings and shouted out with amazement as each strenuous movement of the ship. Young Yseult, the Novice, seemed excited rather than anxious. Her "woooah!" or "aaaaweh!" at each sudden dip or lurch, with laughter and smiles, indicated either deep faith in Providence or an irresponsible levity.

Sister Amise, plump and solid, was untypically quiet and unsmiling. Usually, her joviality disguised whatever her real nature was thinking and feeling but now that helpful mask deserted her. Her usual ruddy complexion was now tinged with green alternating with greyish pallor.

Alongside them were the three servant-girls who had enjoyed the company of the troops. They were young and sturdy, and all with braided blond hair in the old Viking manner. The backward farming communities from which they came had largely kept their Scandinavian heritage. Their rough Norman French was richly interspersed with words and phrases from their Nordic roots. They swore loudly at every violent movement. One even fell off the bench and decided to laugh uproariously as her legs waved and clogs flew off her feet. Opposite them were two more mature servants, including Eulalia's own personal servant, Margot, a comfortable matron of great good sense and loyalty, whose strong rural dialect Eulalia could barely understand. Margot had joined Eulalia's service when the latter had been appointed sub-Prioress at Caen, the year before. All Sisters at the Abbey of the Trinity, founded by King William's devout wife, Matilda of Flanders, were allowed their own personal maids when they achieved that degree of seniority, rather than just the general servants shared by all. They also had the privilege of separate cubicles instead of sleeping on mattresses on long planks in the dormitories, with the Abbess even possessing her own house.

Eulalia: Leadership at Sea

As the Sisters, my closest friends, were suffering from the cold, wet and violent motion, I felt my conscience stir. Was I wrong to put their lives at risk like this? Should I not have come alone on this journey, with perhaps a knight or two to protect me, without these vulnerable women? Will we be met by the Abbey's priest and an armed escort, as we have been promised? Would there not be sufficient numbers of Saxon nuns to meet the needs of the community of the great abbey I was to head? Every groan and whimper from my fellow Religious as they suffered, caused more pain in my heart.

I could not look at the Sisters either side of me, as one was almost constantly retching, and another called almost hysterically on the Good God to save them all. While I agreed with the sentiment, I felt it unhelpful to hear it repeated quite so often and so loudly. A calming of nerves was still needed.

They look to me for leadership, I told myself. I have to be strong for them. Not easy when I am nauseous, wet, and shivering from cold and fear. Still, it is my fault they are here with this torment and I am the one called to lead them. St Mary, St Elfgivu, St Edward, help me! My good patron Queen Matilda encouraged me to foster devotion to royal Saxon saints, as she did with St Cuthbert in the north of the realm. Good religion — and good politics, she said. Oh how I will miss her wise and mature judgement in all things. No wonder our King William leaves her in charge of affairs in his absence.

I observed the sailors, grim but silent, and the merchants seated facing me on benches further along beneath the curved brow, pale but impassive. One man wore pagan talismen around his neck which he touched with just-kissed fingertips at critical moments. The others, their hands anxiously steadying the large leather boxes, were dressed in robes of an exotic eastern style, probably, I surmised, coming from the Byzantine Empire, possibly even so far as Armenia. So extensive was the mighty new Norman

Empire! I smiled with pride but then remembered where I was heading — land of the recently defeated Saxons. What was I to find?

The ship suddenly lurched over to an angle that seemed to defy the laws of nature. A few moments later it righted itself. The occupants, even the experienced oarsmen, all breathed out with relief that they had not been tossed overboard into the dark green waters.

"Look at them," I called out and indicated to my Sisters to observe the men aboard.

In the steadiest voice I could muster, trying not to betray my own considerable anxiety, I directed them, "Look at these men at their oars. They are not screaming and fussing. And the merchants too, at the other end. See. They are not even Christians, yet they are not afraid. Neither should you be, my Sisters. Was not our Lord Jesus caught in a storm and did he not bring his disciples safely to land? Come, come. Let us say together the Pater and hold each other's hands for comfort."

As the day darkened, I felt I could do no more but pray and hope.

Chronicle: Dry Land

All night the gale roared, stinging the women's faces with salty spray and floating snow-clouds of spume as they tried, largely unsuccessfully, to catch some sleep. At dawn the storm suddenly moderated, the waves grew smaller, but a chilling wind still blew. By the following midmorning the ship, having made progress despite the exhaustion of the crew, was in sight of the English coast but seemingly far west of the Wessex port of their destination. Heartened at the sight of land, the master made the decision to turn about, ship the oars and unfurl the sail, letting the westerly wind drive the ship. That was a tactical mistake, despite being a relief for the exhausted oarsmen. So strong was the wind still that the ship sailed on past her intended destination, the harbour of Melcombe Regis (Weymouth). That was where Sir Bertin, Chaplain to Shaftesbury Abbey, was waiting with a squad of soldiers to accompany the nuns to their new home. He was not best pleased to see the billowing striped sail of the knarr still some distance out in the channel heading east at speed.

Then, just as quickly as it had blown up, the wind subsided, the sea barely rippling, and the ship was able to be steered towards the coast. Narrowly avoiding treacherous rocky outcrops, it rounded a headland where it fetched up safely on a sandy beach at Studland Bay.

"God is with us!" rose from every nunnish mouth.

"And all thanks no doubt to the intercession of Saint Queen Elfgivu!" reminded the Abbess-elect.

With impressive good fortune they had landed on territory belonging to Robert, Count of Mortain, half-brother to King William himself, and full brother to the nuns' dear friend Earl Odo, the fabulously wealthy Bishop of Bayeux and frequent Regent in Normandy.

The captain was an obliging fellow, commanding some of his oarsmen to carry the women from the ship onto the beach so that their habits or skirts would not be further soaked. The crew's legs just got wet. As the female passengers assembled on the sand, their luggage was unloaded and formed into piles and guarded by the young servant-girls, until it would be collected. Inquisitive seagulls pecked at the bundles and mewed and screeched in alarm and annoyance as they were chased away. The merchant men continued on board, as they were bound for the trading port of Hamwic (Southampton) further to the east

With shaky legs, the Sisters followed the captain's directions and forced themselves up a hill path leading to level ground. They trudged across fields to the shelter of the ruined shell of an old Saxon church, destroyed by the Danes some years before. It had crumbling walls, but no roof — poor shelter, but at least they were out of the chilly west wind. (This was the church that Count Robert later rebuilt fully in the Norman fashion, and dedicated to St Nicholas, patron of seafarers). They sat on whatever stones offered enough flat surface, or else on the ground, leaning their backs on walls which, while not comfortable, at least did not rock and sway and cause water to spray over them. After rest, and with some of the food and water retrieved from their luggage, they were flooded with a sense of peace and relief. They were safe, at least from the elements. What of the locals, though? How would they react to an unaccompanied party of Norman women? What were they to do now, as their Chaplain was not to be seen?

However, after a time, a friendly group of Norman workmen showed up at the church led by a beaming gentleman who introduced himself, with every courtesy, as Count Robert's steward, Sir Hugh of St Malo. Dame Eulalia rose to greet him, relieved to hear his educated Norman accent. He was spending the day on the beach at Studland Bay overseeing the salt panning and making arrangements to transport that precious commodity to towns and monasteries in the area.

With good grace he guided the party towards the industrial area along the beach to where their luggage had been moved. Their three young servants greeted them as if they had been parted for weeks not less than an hour! As they looked around the salt works, he delighted in explaining how the Romans centuries before had developed the saltern and some of their equipment had still been in use very recently. Shards of their flat drying pans still littered the sand above the tideline.

Steward Hugh beamed with pride while recounting details of his profitable innovation, replacing ceramic with iron, and then left the women admiring the kilns and pans while he went to fetch transport. They watched with interest while the salt workers poured white crystals into sacks, and fed the the fire in the kilns with kindling. The men kept their heads down to give the impression of working hard, while snatching sheepish looks up at the young females. Two youths giggled nervously until cuffed by an older labourer, who then crossed himself and apologised to the Good Sisters on behalf of his apprentices. "Saxons!" he shrugged, as if that explained everything.

From a cluster of wooden shacks, festooned with fishing nets, Sir Hugh appeared, waving at the women to join him across the sand. On firmer ground, where sparkling mounds of salt crystals formed shining heaps, men were holding the bridles of riding horses and leading reins of carthorses attached to sturdy vehicles. Soon the party's luggage was installed on the transport, such as it was — rough wooden carts sprinkled with salt granules and smelly from the residue of leaky barrels of fish liquid. Their belongings were joined by the older sisters, lifted there by strong male arms. The other nuns mounted, rather disdainfully, the Saxon ponies, creatures of no more than twelve hands in height. Norman breeds were more elegantly tall.

Sir Hugh and Dame Eulalia rode in front of the others with the carts trailing behind. During their ride the steward entertained the Abbess-elect with anecdotes from his life in service to his noble lord. He made her forget her hunger, cold and bone-aches with his humour and fascinating insights into court life. The point of view of an intelligent man provided novelty and freshness to one who was familiar only with the company of high-born women.

"Such an amiable and courteous man is this Sir Hugh", she considered. "A true Norman gentleman!"

Eulalia: *Corfe*

After about two to three hours, largely crossing heathland and following forest trails, darkness fell. We arrived at Corfe Hall, perched atop a steep hill, and were given a warm welcome by Count Robert himself and his charming wife, Matilda of Montgomery.

"Dear Sisters", he said smiling at our breathlessness for

we had dismounted, "this is nothing compared to the hill on which your abbey sits!"

After a welcome hot meal served with good Frankish wine, Count Robert and Lady Matilda's young daughters, Emma and Agnes, entertained us weary travellers with songs, while baby William, after being passed from lap to lap, gurgled charmingly until, looking up at Sister Alicia's curled lip of distaste, he began to cry and was quickly removed by his wetnurse. At the appropriate time, we said our prayers, and we and our servants retired for the night.

The next morning, as dawn was breaking, I and my Sisters were awakened by the noise of stonemasons hammering and shouting as they worked. The din rose up from all around the hilltop as workers constructed outer walls of what would become an imposing castle. This noise would become familiar to us all here in Shaftesbury, since we too have embarked on an impressive and ambitious building project.

At Corfe, the timber Great Hall in which visitors had been welcomed, while sturdy and spacious — as a royal house should be — would eventually be demolished once the new stone castle was ready. As we had arrived in the gloom of night and with tired eyes, we were not aware that the Hall and the guest hall annexed to it where we slept, was in the middle of a building site. In the few years since the Conquest, we Normans have been building on a scale never seen since the Roman occupation of this land. Castles and church buildings are rising to the sky and as solid as rock. They declare for all to see that a superior civilisation has arrived — and is here for ever.

We travellers from Caen joined Count Robert's family in breaking our night-fast with bread, and cheese specially brought over from Normandy, and plenty of watery ale.

"There is such a quantity of ale over here that good Norman cider and wine are drunk only at feasts and special meals," explained the Count. I considered then that if I were to exist happily in my Saxon abbey, I would have to plant orchards of Norman tannic cider-apples and vineyards of French grapes.

Over the table Count Robert told me that Corfe had once long been the property of Shaftesbury Abbey, but that Duke William had made a deal with my predecesor, the Abbess Leveva, to exchange Corfe for the Minster church at the settlement of Gillingham, known for its many flour mills, near to Shaftesbury and set within a royal hunting forest. That meant little to me as the only Gillingham of which I had heard was the one in the southeast of the land, with its grand palace for Bishop Odo, the Earl of Kent.

Count Robert, Odo's brother, went on to explain that Corfe was the site of the martyrdom, a hundred years before, of the famous Saxon saint, King Edward. As a king, he was not politically astute, in fact he was rather weak and could not prevent some nobles from robbing and dispossessing various Benedictine abbeys and monasteries during his reign. Of course, he was only a youth and had not yet reached full manhood. When he met his cruel and untimely death at the hands of his stepmother the young King became widely known and acclaimed as a miracle-working Saint and Martyr.

"Oh, that Edward!" I realised then of whom the Count was speaking — so confusing when all Saxon names tend to be Ed- or Eth- something. "He who is buried at Shaftesbury Abbey?"

"Indeed, the one," pronounced the Count with satisfaction. "Both Archbishops, Dunstan of Canterbury and Oswald of York, had favoured the youth over his half-brother Ethelred, who usurped the crown after his mother had the young king murdered — right here, at Corfe."

I shuddered to think of such a barbarous act committed on this spot and was so deeply imagining the scene of the crime that I barely attended to the Count's history lesson.

"Ethelred", he was saying, "has been nicknamed the 'Unred'. That's a pun, you know in English as 'Ethel-red' in the Saxon tongue means nobly or well advised and he was most 'poorly advised'." He laughed.

So that is what passes here for verbal humour, I thought and forced a smile.

"Anyway," he continued, oblivious. My thoughts had moved on. I was considering the journey that lay ahead when Robert's voice broke through.

"So then," he was saying, "after he was killed, Edward's body was hidden by the culprits in the hovel of an old blind woman, someone who would not be able to talk about the wicked deed. However, when his friends came to find him *next day, the old crone had miraculously recovered her sight. Obviously, God had heard the young saint's pleas in heaven to grant this boon. So, the story of King Edward's healing power soon spread throughout Christendom, and now they all flock to his tomb at Shaftesbury."*

Now my attention was fully taken. "Go on," I urged. I had not realised that my future abbey was so sought-after by pilgrims.

"Well, his body was then taken first to Wareham Priory — where I suggest you go straight after leaving here — where it was temporarily buried, and a year later, with great ceremony, carried to your abbey where he lies near his sainted grandmother Queen Elfgiva. His fame has rather eclipsed hers, but both attract pilgrims."

"These pilgrims...?" My mind raced. Devotions such as pilgrimages must be promoted and developed. By honouring the holy dead, the saints who pray for us in heaven, they bless those who approach their sacred relics. The faithful who pray through them are healed of their infirmities, or are delivered from cruel demons. They find that which is lost or have their loved ones relieved of suffering. Besides, the gratitude of pilgrims results in great wealth for the sites wherein the relics rest. I foresaw this Shaftesbury Abbey as a famous destination throughout Europe, profitable both materially and spiritually, setting it above all others. It would be my duty to develop it, obviously.

I admit to a moment of annoyance. To have possessed both sites of a pilgrimage route, Corfe at the start, where the martyrdom was committed, and the abbey at the end where his sainted bones have their home, would have given us a great advantage. But that Abbess Leveva must have been weak or stupid to squander it, trading it in for, what? the church at Gillingham! But no matter. It is done, I am resigned. Corfe is lost to us, so we must concentrate on our end of the pilgrim route. So were my thoughts, but I then caught words from the Count that deepened my vexation.

"So revered is this saint," he was saying, "that the Saxons actually called the town where your abbey is, 'Edwardstowe'. No doubt", he laughed, as he added, "the Latin name 'Sceptesberiensis' proved too difficult for them to say!"

I found Count Robert an hospitable host, but like many great men, he does assume his every thought and word to be of immense value. I later heard, and hope it is not true, that he would beat his wife with great violence, the mild and delightful Matilda de Montgomery who seemed to me the most harmless of women, despite being a daughter of the notorious House of Bellême. Her mother, the Countess of Shrewsbury, was notorious for many evil and wicked acts of cruelty and murder. However, it is best not to dwell on this, as the Count did kindly provide us with a retinue of soldiers, horses and carts. Moreover he ordered his steward Hugh of St Malo to be our guide and companion, much to my satisfaction.

Wareham

Shortly after leaving Corfe, we arrived at Wareham, where we visited the house of the Lady St Mary Priory, the home of monks from the Norman Abbey of Saint-Wandrille de Fontenelle. Wareham is a damp place between two rivers, the Piddle and the Frome, which run down into the sea at Poole. I did not care for it at all, despite our Abbey owning large parts of the area.

To the gatekeeper, a surly old monk, whose deformed spine caused him to stoop, I explained our acquaintance with the abbot of their mother house back in Normandy. He did not move or say a word. Then Hugh, in a firm tone, delivered Count Robert's formal address of introduction. The man then grunted and drew back the bolts, giving us access.

While a troop of servants silently brought us refreshment, Hugh quietly explained the situation here. Founded nearly two hundred years ago by King Alfred as a fortified town, a burh, with its high earthen ramparts still existing, it had once been graced by a great abbey, destroyed by Danes and rebuilt. Yet this later one itself had been dissolved nearly a hundred years ago, through poor management and a lack of religious zeal. The smaller priory, in which we were, had previously been a minster church, of some wealth, until presented to the ancient Benedictine abbey in Normandy as an outpost. Now it served a purpose, but it did not inspire me.

We attended Mass with the half-dozen monks, who were civil but not warm in their welcome. They would not look any of us women in the face but addressed themselves solely to Hugh. He said that was because they feared that all women could lead them to thoughts of sin. Heavens! Half of us are aged over thirty! I suspect that living among unfriendly Saxons has eroded whatever good humour they had once possessed and dampened their spirits. I must not let that happen to us in Shaftesbury. These monks allow no laywomen ever to enter and only took us and our servants because of their duty to Count Robert. After prayers, we left as soon as was polite.

For three days we travelled through all manner of terrain — crossing marshy swamps and deep forests, fording rivers and rattling over fields on ancient muddy tracks. Our lack of speed allowed us fully to observe the landmarks and landscapes through which we passed. Some were similar to our Norman countryside, but much was not. The villages and hamlets were different. So many of the humble buildings were of wood, as that is plentiful in this country, with the thatches poorly maintained, and the cottagers' hens and geese churning up the mud around their hovels.

The occupants stared at us unsmiling as we passed. Children ran to hide in their mothers' skirts, and even the dogs seemed too awed to bark at us. Some of the men turned their backs on us, and one youth even threw a stone towards a cart. Two of our soldiers caught and beat him suitably. A broken arm should deter him in future from such behaviour. The occasional Norman house or church, newly hewn in stone and rising above the Saxon hovels, was acknowledged by our cheerful cries of 'Look there!' and 'God be praised!'. Hugh of St Malo proved an efficient guide, having made the same journey on several occasions in the service of his master.

Thanks to the generosity of Count Robert our next two resting places, where we passed the hours of darkness being well entertained and comfortably lodged, both belonged to him. Hugh was instantly recognised by our hosts, with beaming smiles and obvious delight. This ensured we were admitted and welcomed by the tenants of the great houses in Winterborne Kingston, the first night, and Child Okeford, the next. Winterborne lived up to its name, the King's village where the river ran full in wintertime but was dry in the summer. Approaching the swollen river Stour we feared we would be stranded on one side. But Hugh knew where there was a sturdy wooden bridge over which we clattered.

We spent a short time in Shillingstone, where the Norman Lord, Azeline, provided us with gifts of food and wine, before going on to nearby Okeford. Count Robert's tenant there was kindness itself. He requested prayers from us in exchange for a regular supply of cider for the abbey, until our own Norman cider-apple trees are grown. He would provide the seedlings, he promised.

From Okeford then, in pouring rain and with the poor

horses enduring many steep hills, we finally reached Shaftesbury.

Chronicle: Arriving in Shaftesbury

The Sisters' first sight of the town depressed them. It was a miserable place, with many burnt-out or knocked-down shells of houses like missing teeth in a jaw. Of the two hundred and fifty or so houses which had at one time stood, belonging to either the Abbey or the King, some eighty-five had been destroyed as punishment, we later learnt, for resisting Norman rule.

The people stood silently at their doors regarding the convoy as they rode by or stared out through their glass-less windows. Most of the houses were of roughly-hewn stone, with still a few built of wood and thatch. Many were obviously designed to accommodate visitors such as pilgrims and tradesmen, and there were several compact chapels.

A welcoming party met the incomers on the main street, Bimport, led by the thick-set Sheriff Arnold Fitzgrip, the King's Reeve and representative in the shire. The Sheriff possessed a commanding presence, and a scar 'of honour' across his ruddy cheek from a wound which had almost cost him the loss of an eye.

He stood beaming at the arrivals with such confidence that it lightened their hearts.

Those on horseback dismounted with the help of serving men who rushed to their aid, as the Sheriff and Hugh de Malo embraced as old friends, for indeed they had been fellow warriors in arms in several battles, including the great battle at Hastings. Such military experiences, when each other's lives depend upon their mutual support and loyalty, creates great bonds, so they say.

Sheriff Fitzgrip introduced Sir Thibault de Granville to Dame Eulalia. This finely-dressed gentleman with upright bearing and eyes bright with intelligence had been newly appointed by King William as the Abbey's High Steward, being an honest man by reputation, and a highly efficient accountant. Modestly waving away such flattery, Sir Thibault's greeting was replete with pleasing courtesy, although perhaps his manner lacked the sincerity and innate good humour of Sir Hugh of St Malo. A Norman, though married to a Saxon lady, Thibault, with his staff, would be working closely together with the Abbess, the Cellaress and the Prioress on running the Abbey's extensive estate. A flourishing abbey needs healthy finances, as well as deep devotion and sound Benedictine principles. Sir Thibault invited the Abbess-elect to dine with him and the other lay notables that evening, as their wives desired the pleasure of meeting her.

The laymen and the armed escort withdrew, taking charge of the riding horses, leaving the Sisters and their carts to enter through the gatehouse and advance towards the church to give thanks to God for their safe arrival. Several servants stood around the open space between the buildings ready to unpack and dispose of the goods on the wagons.

This Abbey of St Mary and St Edward was reputed to be the wealthiest nunnery in England, owning over three hundred and fifty hides locally and others further afield, and with assets of nearly three hundred pounds. And yet the first impressions of the buildings were that they had been greatly neglected. Thatches needed repair and fallen plaster revealed patches of the mud and wattle beneath. Even the stumpy stone buildings and walls were shabby, with weeds and mosses growing on them, and mould blackening their northerly faces. Hardly the magnificent stone edifices of the Norman abbey the ladies had just left. Quite disheartening.

The Abbess-elect could see at once that a programme of good stone building work was urgently needed. From glorious beginnings when the Abbey was founded, two hundred years before, religious life — just as with secular life — had suffered much from endless generations of violent invasions and warfare. Vikings such as King Cnut, who died in this very Abbey, may have converted to Christianity and repaired some of the harm they had brought down upon monasteries and abbeys, yet their previous destructions and pillages had left their mark. The nearby Cerne Abbey was just one example of this. Cnut had first almost destroyed it, then lavished donations and other attempts to restore the holy place.

From the church emerged a large group of Saxon women, some in black habits, others in their own clothes. They stopped as their Norman counterparts drew closer. One, a slight, rather wizened older woman habited as a nun, stepped forward. She singled out Dame Eulalia and addressed her in halting Norman French. Through tight lips and with barely concealed hostility she muttered,

'Welcome, Sisters. I am Acting-Prioress Eadifu. As Abbess Leveva was shamefully sent away from here with her Prioress and the other Obedientes, her most senior nuns, I have been chosen to lead this community until your arrival. If there is anything you or your Sisters need, you must ask one of us, but you will find that they might not understand you. We speak only English here."

Eulalia took some time to process the Prioress's message. The meaning was clear. They hated them — Saxon loathing of Norman hegemony had imbued even this house of religion. The impulse to suddenly turn and leave, to return to her beloved Abbey of the

Trinity at Caen seized her. By the act of restraining tears and praying inwardly, Eulalia fought to overcome this temptation and simply looked away as the Saxons dispersed. Turning to her own dear Norman nuns, she gently urged them not to be dispirited, but to accept the will of God at being in this place and directed them to pray quietly in the small church until her return.

She then hailed the services of some of the abbey servants. She directed her goods be taken to the abbess's house and oversaw the disposition of the rest of their luggage. Eulalia then joined her Sisters in a short *Te Deum* service in the chapel. They gave thanks for their safe arrival, but felt anything but grateful for what they found as they arrived. Even in the darkness relieved only by a few beeswax candles Eulalia could make out the glistening of tears on the cheeks of some of her expatriate Sisters, and groaned inwardly.

"Lord, what have you done to us? How can we live amid this ill-feeling and in these mean buildings? Give us your strength, Lord, or we are done for."

When they left, Sir Hugh and Sheriff Fitzgrip were waiting to accompany Eulalia to enjoy the hospitality of Steward Thibault, while the rest of the Norman nuns trooped off to the refectory to be fed by their Saxon Sisters. That was to be their misfortune.

Eulalia: Dining on the first night

My life was saved the first night of my arrival. God wanted me to accomplish my mission, it appeared.

I went to dine in the company of Sir Hugh of St Malo before he was to return the next day to Count Robert at Corfe. We were hosted by Sir Thibault in his substantial stone house at the east end of Bimport, and also present was Sheriff Fitzgrip. Their wives were introduced to me and I was courteous. Opposite them, on the two tables running from the top table towards the entrance, were worthies from the town — Saxons who had accepted the new status quo and were considered reliable burghers (or collaborating traitors, according to the point of view of many of their neighbours). I noticed that while the Norman gentlemen, even when they were sitting, wore swords slung from their belts, none of the Saxons was armed.

The meal was substantial and the wine very palatable. Having already drunk a little too much, and continuing to raise his goblet, Sheriff Fitzgrip leaned over Sir Hugh towards me to offer this caution,

"Beware the Saxons! Beware of their system of justice, for it lies in — revenge."

I confess I was a little shaken by this, especially remembering Sister Eadifu's implicit detestation of all things Norman.

Embarrassed by the behaviour of his old friend in arms,

Sir Hugh pushed the Sheriff back in his place. Turning to me, Sir Hugh explained quietly, in a reassuring tone,

"They have a system of assessing a person's value, their 'wergild', to calculate how much to give in compensation for violent crimes committed against them. This was a good thing, designed to put an end to the cycle of revenge killings, but the notion of revenge is still deeply ingrained in them. They still believe that deaths and injuries should be avenged."

I was not much comforted, when just then Sheriff Fitzgrip leaned towards me once more, with his elbow in Sir Hugh's stomach, and declared loudly, as if in jest,

"Don't be surprised, my dear Lady Abbess, if some of the Saxons try to kill you just for being Norman!"

While Sir Hugh shushed him and appealed to the Sheriff's Lady to take him in hand and make him sober, Sir Thibault my host, beside me in the centre of the High Table, in a tone of sadness, launched into a tale that did little to calm my fears. My mouth had dried, so I took some sips of wine.

"The Abbess Leveva and her Council were sent away by order of the King. They have been exiled to an obscure convent somewhere in the North, where she had come from. As you may know, she and several other Sisters here were caught up just a few years ago, harbouring rebels, well, refugees really, from the North. King William was obliged to lay waste to the North, killing most of the people and livestock, burning grain stores and basically teaching them a

severe lesson not to rebel against his rule. Hundreds of starving survivors came south — the Abbey at Evesham took in many. Those who could, came further south, even here in some cases. The Abbess gave them shelter and fed them from the Abbey's reserves of food. Most were so weak when they arrived that they did not survive, and some brought disease with them, as well as a deep resentment of us, but the Abbess felt she could not turn them away. They were her own people. When my predecessor, as Reeve, heard of this, he reported the Abbess to the King. In his fury he exiled her. Now he has chosen you, My Lady, to take her place and restore good Norman rule in these parts — but it may take time yet. Do not be discouraged."

I was rendered silent. My mind a tumult of feelings and opinions — one moment approving my predecessor's actions as Christian and charitable, and the next revolting at her disobedience to her King and collaborating with his enemies.

After a moment, Sir Thibault continued,

"Sheriff Fitzgrip and a company of Norman soldiers had to escort Abbess Leveva, along with her senior Sisters, off the Abbey premises, all of them weeping piteously. Mobs of townspeople gathered along Bimport and beyond to jeer and lob stones and abuse at us. Some went on to set fire to sticks and threw them onto the thatch of the barracks, which would have burnt down completely had a sudden rainstorm not prevented it. God protects the good, after all."

"How dreadful," I uttered, shocked.

"These unruly townsfolk shouted that they would resist

'the Norman yoke' as they put it. Well, we had to put down the rebellion in the strongest way, which is how one third of the houses in the town had to be destroyed. You saw that when you arrived. A lesson had to be taught as they were where the worst offenders lived. My men either burnt or pulled them down. Even the houses belonging to you as Abbess here, forty-two of them were destroyed and only one hundred and eleven still stand. A score of properties remain empty, but we'll find good Norman folk or friendly Saxons to fill them, never fear."

The Sheriff, by now drunk beyond all efforts to subdue him, stood up shakily, and roared towards his host,

"Tell her about that bastard Hereward in the East! Tell her what he and his Saxon pigs and Danish mates did at the Abbey at Peterborough! We replaced his uncle Brand as Abbot by a good Norman...They sacked it! Robbed it bare! Then...."

"No, no!" commanded Thibault, to no effect. Sheriff Fitzgrip was warming to his tale.

"Ah, yes, don't stop me. The Saxon thugs then used another Abbey, the one at Ely, as a refuge. Barricaded themselves in it, they did, while we laid it siege. If only the timber causeway — it was a mile long over the marshes — hadn't given way under our weight of horse and armour, we'd have had them!"

I could hardly bear to listen to this series of outrages against holy abbeys, especially as I had barely set foot in my own yet and did not know the full extent of the hostility I would find there.

Fitzgrip could not stop. With slurred words he yelled even more horror stories of the recent past,

"Then we used the witch. Remember her? From the top of a wooden tower she poured curses upon Hereward and his barbarians. So what did they do? Just set fire to the tower and burnt it up along with the witch! Huh!"

He subsided onto his bench, overcome suddenly by sleep and, leaning his head upon his wife's bosom, began snoring loudly, slobbering over her bliaut (bodice).

Sir Hugh, turning his back on the drunkard, quietly resumed the account.

"One of the monks showed Sir Belsar, one of our knights, how to cross the treacherous marshland of the Fens and safely approach the Isle of Ely. A contingent of our men then took back the Abbey and captured many of the rebels."

"And Hereward?" I asked.

"Ah, unfortunately not. The brute is still at large somewhere, but has not been heard of anymore, so there is no real threat."

I felt distinctly unimpressed by this assurance.

Chronicle: A Tragic Death

Sir Bertin, the Abbey's Chaplain, had been a secular married canon in Exeter Cathedral since it was founded in 1050, but after his wife had died, was feeling tired of the routine of life there. When King William appointed him to Shaftesbury and charged him with preparing the place for their Norman Abbess, a new surge of vitality gripped him. Life looked better. He had spent an awkward couple of months in the company of the Saxon nuns until he received word that the new Abbess and several Sisters would shortly be arriving at Melcombe Regis. He set off there with a squad of soldiers from the Shaftesbury barracks which adjoined the abbey.

Several days later, the same day as the arrival of the Norman nuns, he returned to the Abbey at about midnight, having made laborious progress from the port at which he had expected to meet and then accompany the nuns. He had waited until the following day, in case the vessel carrying them had turned back to the designated meeting place. When it did not, he went first to Abbotsbury Abbey, then enjoyed more Benedictine hospitality at the Abbey of Cerne and then at that of Milton before journeying all day and half the night to Shaftesbury, stopping off wherever ale or bread could be procured. With a plump figure and red face Sir Bertin conveyed an impression of amiability and good humour, which however harboured a calculating mind and ability to detect any opportunity which he could use to his personal advantage. On arrival, he forwent any further meals, called in at the chapel for brief prayers of thanks for his safe arrival, and went to his quarters, settling at once to sleep.

Wakened at dawn by loud exclamations. Women's voices clamoured for him, in Norman French, to "Come at once!" He threw on his cloak, forced his feet into his shoes, but neglected to close them above his ankles with the leather thongs, and hurried outside. There, lit only by moonlight, were two distraught black-clad nuns. One tugged at his cloak to pull him towards the hospital block.

"Come quickly, Sir Bertin. Please, she's fading fast!"

Inside the dark and fetid timber building, tapers and candles dropped pools of light, mainly upon one bed in which an elderly nun was dying. He saw her half-closed eyes and gagged at the stench of vomit around her pillow. He steeled himself to attend the Sister's last moments, drawing out a small bronze cross from a pouch attached to his belt and holding it before her. While praying and holding the cross in one hand he fumbled in the pouch for a tiny vial of oil. When extracted, he used the liquid contents to anoint her on the forehead, lips and chest, making the sign of the cross on each with his oily thumb.

As she breathed her last, to much wailing from the attendant nuns, Sir Bertin noticed that the adjoining beds were also occupied by nuns, groaning or wincing. Servants and nuns wove between them carrying stinking buckets and towels and flagons of water. After attending to the invalids with noticeably rushed prayers, he gratefully sought the fresh outside air, breathing in deep lungsful as he stumbled his way to the chapel to pray for the recently departed. The Requiem Mass and burial would need to be arranged as soon as possible. This was not the return he had been expecting.

Eulalia: Saxon vs Norman hostility

I have not slept well. The feather and wool mattress on my bed almost collapsed under me as I lay down. The ropes beneath it, stretched from side to side of the bed frame, were loose, causing it to sink beneath my weight. I called my servant Margot from the next room and together we tightened the ropes. They had been deliberately loosened, anyone could see that. How spiteful.

After an hour or two of sleep, I heard a bell toll and assumed it was to summon us for Prime. On rising and stumbling my way to the chapel in the dark, for the moon was overcast and the sun had not yet appeared, I heard, rather than saw, numerous people moving about, hurrying mostly, and some odd noises like little sobs and chokings. There were a few nuns already in the chapel, all Saxon from what I could see by the candlelight. No-one I knew. Then Prioress Eadifu pushed forward towards me and whispered something of which I could make out but few words. Those I heard chilled me.

"What?" I responded. "Ill? All of them? Dead — who is dead?"

"No, no. Not all. Only the old one...."

I demanded to be taken at once to the hospital, and holding onto a candle to light my way, followed the Acting Prioress across the unfamiliar ground. I was met by Margot. The woman's face was distorted with anxiety, and she kept slapping her head with both hands to express the awfulness of what she had to relate.

"Why, Margot, calm yourself, woman!"

"Oh my Lady. They've been poisoned, all of them! Retching and vomiting they are, some fainting and falling down, and old Sister Anne-Marie has gone and passed away!"

I felt sudden nausea rising and clutched my own tightened throat. "I know, Margot, but what exactly happened? Tell me as we go."

Margot explained that the newly arrived Sisters and their servants were provided with a hot evening meal of simple vegetable and barley stew prepared by the Saxon Sisters.

"It tasted bitter, but we all assumed that was just the Saxon way. We knew they were not good cooks, that's well known. We ignored the funny taste. Well, my tummy was still upset after that awful sea crossing and the bumpy wagon all those days coming overland, so I just had a very small amount, and nearly spat it out. A bit of bread was all I wanted."

I, half running, half walking, arrived at the infirmary where several of my nuns were still noisily groaning and vomiting. Servants and Saxon Sisters were running in and out with buckets and cloths. I fell to my knees beside the covered and still body of my old friend and prayed for her eternal soul.

When dawn broke, I left, supported by Margot's strong arm in mine. I was met at the steps of the infirmary by Sir Hugh of St Malo and Sir Thibault who had heard the news of the suffering nuns and had hurried round. Alternating expressions of anger and commiserations they swore to root out the poisoning culprits and punish them severely.

"No, please don't interfere," I insisted. "I can't have the Sisters interrogated by outsiders. We'll do it ourselves here, gentlemen. I'm sure confessions will be forthcoming once we Normans have gained their trust. Sister Anne-Marie, God-bless-her-soul, was very old when she came, well over sixty, and weakened by the journey. I think she might not have survived anyway. I had not wanted her to come, but she insisted. Poor stubborn old soul. She will be buried as soon *as our Chaplain can arrange it. I understand he attended her at the end."*

I prattled on to calm myself, when Sir Hugh mentioned the investigation of a new royally-appointed officer, a 'coroner'.

"When a Norman dies in suspicious circumstances where Saxons may be responsible, this officer is summoned to seek out the facts, the truth. The sheriff then prosecutes and punishes the wrongdoer."

I refused the offer, begged that no such interrogator be summoned. I was convinced that no Saxon Religious woman would ever have intended to kill poor harmless old Sister Anne-Marie.

"Please, we'll call it natural causes, and leave it to me to find out who, if anyone, put poison in their food last night, if that is what happened. Meanwhile, gentlemen, I need to find my Chaplain, whom I have not yet met."

Sir Bertin and I made arrangements for the funeral and spent much of the rest of the day in the chapel praying vocally and in silence. By the end of the day all but one of the surviving Sisters had recovered, although they felt wary of their Saxon counterparts.

Sister Suzanna was the one patient remaining very weak for several days. Her being simple-minded did not help, as she rejected the good broths and herbal infusions (made by safe Norman hands) that would have aided her recovery. All she took was ale and morsels of bread. For my protection, for several weeks I made my servant Margot stay awake all night to guard me. She sleeps during the day, but then she always did.

I ordered that the two groups, Saxon and Norman, were to be separated for sleeping and eating, and that Normans were to be represented in the kitchen at all times of food preparation. I would, in time, discover the culprits if poisoning had been deliberate. What to do with them required thought and prayerful discernment. I had still had not met the Saxon nuns and was very careful that only Margot was to prepare my food.

I thought about poor Sister Anne-Marie for many days whenever I sat in silent meditation or lay down to sleep. She had been my Novice Mistress when I first entered Trinity Abbey in 1062, shortly after it was founded, and she had been gentle with me, knowing how shy and withdrawn I was as a seventeen-year-old. Before entering I had attended a small convent for a few months to learn my letters and numbers, but my education at home had been mainly learning how to pluck and gut poultry, skin rabbits and generally knowing what the servants did in order to command them when I had a household of my own. Of course, like all girls, I learnt how to card wool and spin it, weave and sew, and embroider on silk.

With some others in the novitiate, I was taken to the new men's Abbey of St Stephen, (jointly founded with the women's Trinity Abbey, by Duke William and Matilda) to be shown how vellum and parchment were scraped and stretched. We were allowed to draw lines on them, in preparation for being written on. The monks in the Scriptorium then taught us how to copy and even how to illustrate certain letters. The Prior, Lanfranc, lent us many books and scrolls and encouraged us to read as much and as widely as we could.

Between the two great abbeys at Caen I received a good education. In the novitiate, Sister Anne-Marie had sat beside me for many hours teaching me to read the Latin Scriptures and how to sing the chants and responses. She accompanied us to St Stephen's Abbey and assisted Prior Lanfranc in choosing our reading material.

She was known for her patience with all the youngsters, but as she grew older, began to tolerate their silliness less, becoming infuriated with the giggling and whisperings the girls, barely out of childhood, indulged in when they thought themselves alone.

In her old age, she began to cling to fixed ideas and was not willing to listen to reason, such as when Abbess Matilda and I tried to dissuade her from making the arduous journey over water to this Saxon Abbey. She had the strong idea that the Saxon nuns here needed her guidance and wisdom. Yet had she not come, she might still be alive. If only I had been firmer and refused her, but it seemed unnatural to contradict the wishes of one older than oneself and who had been such an influence on my own development as a

Benedictine. Who would have known that the malice of a Sister in Christ could have caused the death of this harmless soul? I shall find the culprit out, and maybe do so with heavenly guidance from Sister Anne-Marie — whose time in purgatory must surely be brief.

Chronicle: Responsibilities and general impressions

The following morning Sir Bertin led a Requiem Mass for Sister Anne-Marie, attended by all the nuns, Saxon and Norman. Sir Hugh and Sir Thibault also attended, looking about them to see if any of the Saxons betrayed their guilt by looking smug. To the men's disappointment, everyone appeared equally morose and sorrowful. Also looking about her was Eulalia. She was checking to see who was present and noticed the absence of several women she had seen within the enclosure who were not attired in Benedictine habit, nor in the dowdy dress of servants or working people.

One in particular had caught her attention. A middle-aged noblewoman, whose name she learnt was Goldiva, had been attired in gaudy colours of fine fabric, and wore a pair of golden shoulder-brooches with several strings of bright blue glass beads between them. The woman had stared at Eulalia with a downturned mouth and hard unswerving eyes that

Eulalia found unsettling, causing a shivering pang down her spine. Religious and well-bred women would have dropped their gaze respectfully: not so Goldiva.

After the obsequies and interment, the Sisters and their guests went into the refectory to eat bread and cheese so breaking their fast from the previous night, a concession allowed them as they were still feeling weak from their recent sickness. Usually only those who laboured broke their nightly fast with morning food.

Eulalia took Bertin, Thibault and Hugh into her house. There she asked the men about these other ladies, neither nuns nor servants. None of them was eager to answer, each looking to the other to explain. Finally, Sir Hugh spoke up,

"They are noblewomen, Madam, related by blood or marriage to the highest in the land — before the Conquest. They have come here, as to other religious houses, for sanctuary — refugees, you might say."

The silence that greeted that explanation was icy.

Sir Thibault tried to explain: "Some of the younger ones were to be married to Norman nobles; it would have helped them to consolidate their claims on Saxon lands and property, but these ungrateful girls chose to come here instead, or to other nunneries."

Too late, he realised the tactlessness of that remark. He had momentarily forgotten that the calling of virginity and to the religious life is the highest to which a woman can aspire. Marriage must always make way for the worthier life. Such women were due honour and respect, not to be called 'ingrates', even if they were not intending to become Sisters.

Dame Eulalia kindly ignored the insinuation and asked, with a frostiness she could not hide, "So, do they pay their way?"

"Well, ah…" he studied his shuffling feet, "some do — these young women avoiding marriage. They bring their dowries. But the older ones, actually, no. Not exactly. They did arrive with whatever they could bring with them — gold plate, jewellery, deeds of land and so forth, but I rather think they intend to take them back when they feel it is safe to leave."

"Safe? Safe under Norman rule — Christian, civilised, law-abiding rule? Or do they expect that we shall leave, be driven out perhaps, to make way for Saxon rule to return?"

Eulalia's anger sent a frisson of fear through the men. She dismissed them, and they were glad to leave.

The Abbess-elect — although not actually elected by her Sisters, but rather appointed by the King — considered that her next duty was to interview and interrogate the Saxon nuns, not to find the culprit of the poisoning, that would come later, but for testing their vocation and seeing what roles they had exercised and for which offices they were suitable.

One day soon she would decide what to do with those lay women who had no intention of taking vows but were simply taking advantage of the nunnery. If they were generous in payment of one sort or another, that could make a difference as to whether they could stay. The support of religious life was a noble duty and would aid to their credit before the Eternal Judge. Religious institutions had to have solid financial underpinning. Not only did they have religious mouths to feed, but there were always dozens more lay dependents, craftspeople and overseers, labourers and, for all new Norman communities, builders, such as masons, carpenters and architects. Charitable acts were also always expected — hospitality to guests, treatment of patients and education of children, not to mention almsgiving to the poor and destitute. A great abbey had great responsibilities and required great wealth to maintain and flourish. Eulalia sighed as she considered how all of that now rested on her shoulders. With hostile natives a difficult job was made much more so. The poisoning of the Sisters, the loosening of her bed ropes, and the look given her by the wealthy Goldiva emphasised that difficulty.

Margot, always within earshot, heard her mistress summon her. Eulalia sent her to Prioress Eadifu to summon all the Saxon Sisters to assemble in the chapter-house where she would interview them one by one. "Oh, and call Sister Cecilia there as I need her to translate." Can she be the only nun in this abbey with a good command of both English and Norman-French?

This intelligent woman, Cecilia, had been brought up in the court of Edward the Confessor, arriving as a young child in 1051 with her parents accompanying Duke William on a visit, and then staying until she had been sent to Caen some six years earlier. She it was whom Dame Eulalia decided would become her Prioress.

While waiting for the bell to signal that all were gathered as commanded, Sir Bertin asked for, and was granted, permission to enter.

"I have heard from the gentlemen, Hugh and Thibault, that they fear they have offended you, Madame." He added, with a twinkle, "They have lived so long outside Normandy that I suppose their language and manner have been coarsened by long contact with Saxons." Eulalia smiled, thinking how gentlemanly the two knights had proved previously.

He then explained to Eulalia that many noble Saxon women had taken refuge in other local abbeys — for example King Edward the Confessor's widow, Edith, was at neighbouring Wilton Abbey, as was "King" Harold's daughter Gunilda. These Saxon royal women, and ones from Scotland too, once installed in other abbeys, are not all used to the discipline of religious life, although some were reasonably devout, so he had heard. While their Norman Abbesses should like their 'refugees' to leave, they feared the local Saxons would be stirred up to revolt. "Besides, if they could be persuaded fully and completely to donate the wealth they brought, that income would help to support everyone." Dame Eulalia's thoughts precisely.

As no sound had yet come from the chapter-house, Bertin regaled Eulalia with an account of a previous abbess at nearby Wilton, Wulfthryth, the sainted mother of another abbess, Saint Edith (so many Edith's!). Apparently Wulfthrith, while a pupil at Wilton Abbey, attracted the lustful attention of King Edgar who promptly abducted her and forced her into a marriage with him. Once their baby was born, Wulfthrith renounced the marriage and placed the infant into the care of the nuns at Wilton. She followed her daughter into the religious community there, becoming the abbess and gaining a great reputation for holiness.

"So, you see, even married women and widows — such as we have here at Shaftesbury — can become spiritual examples and leaders. Do not judge them harshly, Mother, as some may be saints among them."

"That may be, Bertin, but I shall be wary of all the Saxon women, religious and lay, all those within the precinct, until I learn who among them wanted to harm us with their poison. I would expect the fully professed nuns to be so armed with charity as to refuse to engage in such wickedness. But the others, I shudder to think what bitterness they harbour, especially if their beloved menfolk have been killed in battle against our forces, or their families dispossessed, which is almost as bad."

Then the Abbess and her Chaplain walked together to the chapter-house on hearing the sounding of the chapter-bell. Eulalia considered how she could break down this resistance to the Norman presence and occupation. Whether she should use sternness or gentleness, she had not decided. She turned to Sir Bertin as they neared the gathered Saxons:

"Sir Bertin, I understand that the native population here seems to find it difficult to pronounce and speak a language other than their own."

"Oh true! It seems to be a curious mixture of Germanic, Norse and Frisian dialects. Some words from the earlier language, Brittanic, are still used in country areas apparently, and a few Latin words occasionally make an appearance, but only from the educated few."

"Well, I have a task for you," Eulalia said in a tone that accepted no contradiction. "As you have lived in England for many years, in Exeter, I believe, and are fluent in English, I charge you with the duty of teaching Norman French to the Saxon Sisters and lay noblewomen."

"Indeed, I accept with honour. Some I have already made progress with before your arrival, but these are early days. May I suggest that Sir Thibault's Saxon wife, who has been bi-lingual since her childhood, be established in a sort of language school in the gatehouse, to teach the servants and the labourers around the abbey. They will most readily learn from one of their own — only simple things, of course, but to enable them to understand commands and instructions."

"An excellent idea. Two mutually-exclusive languages are not workable in the one institution, especially when the users of one are the rulers and governors of the users of the other." Dame Eulalia's opinion of Sir Bertin was rising from the initial one of resentment and annoyance which she always felt of ordained men who might try to overrule her on grounds of their supposed natural superiority. Sir Bertin seemed to evince suitable respect, so all would be well.

Just before they entered, Eulalia turned again to her Chaplain, and whispered, lest they be overheard by any Saxon, "One more task, Sir, and that is that you convince my fellow Normans to stay. The Sisters are unhappy, and the lay servants particularly anxious, with the atmosphere of animosity here. Being poisoned on arrival," she shuddered, "is not the kind of hospitality they expected or deserved. Yet it is God's will that we have been called here. There is much to do, and I would that they were happy and willing to do it all."

The priest muttered an "Of course, Abbess" as he

bowed his head in humble obedience, much to her satisfaction.

Abbess Eulalia seated herself on the high chair in the centre of the long wall, with the Sisters standing in rows before her, and bowing on her progress to the chair. With Sister Cecilia's help with translating the language and Sir Bertin standing behind her whispering information (such comments as "This one is very devout" or "She is virtuous but incompetent"), she interviewed each of the Saxon Sisters, holding out her hand to be kissed by each as they were dismissed.

After starting with prayers led by the Abbess — a *Pater* and an *Ave*, and invoking a blessing on their gathering and on the business to be done — Eulalia called for a stool to be placed before her, on which each interviewee would be seated in turn. First she called for the senior nuns, whichever of the Obedientes were left after the expulsion of the Abbess Leveva with her leading nuns. They came and stood before her, with Eadifu in their centre, looking truculent. She guessed what was to come, and perched upon the stool as if it were red hot.

"Sister Eadifu,' declared Eulalia with an authoritative tone she assumed for the occasion, while feeling quite nervous. "You are no longer to be the Prioress of this abbey, but from now will be the sub-Prioress, helping Prioress Cecilia here with her duties, especially in governance of your Saxon Sisters. I expect you to lead them in obedience and charity, submitting in all aspects to our rule and, of course, to the Rule of our Founder, Saint Benedict. Who is the Cellaress? That role is of utmost importance and must be in the hands of the most efficient and dedicated of us."

"Step forward, Rowena," commanded a red-faced Eadifu, furious at her demotion.

A tall woman with piercing blue eyes and a scowl approached and sat down. This was Rowena, of the same age as Eulalia, about thirty years. She had held the post of sub-Cellaress almost since her arrival, as she had great experience in her previous life in running the estates of her often-absent father. His sons had all died either in childhood or battle, and it had fallen to the capable daughter to see that the lands were well managed and the kitchens fully provided. Since the Conquest her family's lands were all confiscated and, other than marrying a Norman, the only course for her was to enter a convent. Shaftesbury was fortunate to have acquired her skills and experience. Eulalia, on learning this, decided to promote Rowena to Cellaress, especially as it meant much contact with their Saxon tenants — their freemen, villeins, cottagers and slaves. She would be working closely with Sir Thibault, the High Steward. Sir Bertin thought that a wise move and hinted that, given encouragement, he could turn Rowena's animosity to friendship.

"Now, the Hospitaless, or Hosteller?"

Sister Bega approached, whose considerable height was augmented by her haughty demeanour. She stood as if a cord were pulling the crown of her head upwards. On being asked to sit, she made such a to-do about folding her habit about her that Eulalia and Cecilia raised eyebrows at each other. This high-born Saxon creature had been in charge of the abbey's guests, but Eulalia doubted that any who were not royally titled or churchmen of the most senior rank would receive much of a warm welcome. By questioning, Eulalia discovered that Bega's real interest lay in the care of church vestments and vessels, ornaments and candles. She was thereby appointed Sacrist and responded with a rare smile. The role of Hosteller, Eulalia decided, was to go to Dame Anise of Caen. That Sister's jovial nature and friendliness would make an ideal host for guests, rich and poor, travellers with their retinues and horses.

The role of Infirmaress was next to be appointed. Sister Everilda, an elderly lady with stiff joints spoke quietly through lips tightened with ill-feeling. She it was in charge of the hospital, knowing all there was to know about herbs and potions. She would know about poisons too, thought Eulalia. Neither she nor Cecilia found the old Saxon agreeable, and it was decided that she should be assistant to the Norman nun Adeliza, who had assisted in the hospital at Caen and so knew what to do. The older woman took the demotion badly, hardly refraining from spitting on the hand of her Abbess as she was obliged to kiss it.

Through Cecilia, Sub-Prioress Eadifu requested that another Saxon, Sister Lewina be called forward. Doe-eye and timid, this creature was forever crossing herself and muttering prayers even as she was being questioned. It seemed that her specialism within the community was textiles — embroidery and weaving. In these she was apparently accomplished and had been in charge of the management of the linens, bedding and clothing. "So she shall continue, as Chambress," declared Eulalia.

She was followed by Sister Hilda, smiling nervously and as eager to please as a puppy. She had been Almoness, visiting the poor and providing for the destitute. She could keep that post. Her trustworthiness Eulalia seriously doubted, naturally cynical about obsequious juniors, but the next was even more suspected — the twitchy, skeletal Sister Wunna, who had been in charge of the kitchen and all food preparation. This sister had been in post for that first disastrous meal. Was she the guilty one, the poisoner? She was told to continue providing for the Saxons, but would share the kitchen with the Norman Sister Rotza, who would see to the meals of the Normans until the poisoner could be found.

Just two further Saxon Sisters presented themselves

to be interviewed: Sister Orva, whose strong and tuneful voice apparently led the sisters in singing the psalms at the Offices. She had been Precentor, taking charge of all services and music, including the copying of music manuscripts. However, Abbess Eulalia soon sent for a monk from the Abbey of Cluny, foremost for liturgical excellence, to teach new chants and responses. The Norman Sister Alicia, also a gifted singer and with excellent Latin, would supervise all the Sisters during Masses and Offices, while the manuscript department, running the scriptorium and taking care of the books and archives of the Abbey as the Armarius and Archivist would be the responsibility of Sister Aubrey (myself, the writer of this chronicle). Sister Orva was to be simply a copyist within the scriptorium — a skill in which she became highly proficient.

The last, young Sister Tibba, whose eyes sparkled with intelligence, presented herself. Eulalia and Cecilia warmed to her instantly — especially when they learned that she could, in fact, speak Norman French and was fluent in Latin. Sir Bertin approved of her heartily. She would be in charge of novices and the education of children. Beaming smiles all round.

There were a few Saxon Sisters left, who held either menial roles as assistants or none. These fell under the piercing gaze of the Abbess, and in turn either blushed, or looked away or down to their feet. All were dismissed apart from the new Prioress and her assistant. The Abbess then demanded of them a list of the names and degrees in status of all the other people living within the abbey enclosure, from the noblewomen and their servants, to the humblest craftsperson, slave and labourer, with their families.

Abbess Eulalia stayed alone in the chapter-house until the bell tolled for attendance in the chapel. She needed time to assess the experience she had undertaken, the first of the most important duties of her abbacy.

From what she had seen around her, Eulalia came to realise that for many years these nuns, like all the Saxons, had been more concerned with survival than with anything else, even the rules of the religious life. The revenues from their lands, the harvests and tithes, had all become diminished by the uncertainty of the times. Men had been called from the fields to fight first Vikings and then Normans, and with plagues and poor harvests from unreliable weather or infestations, their surviving tenants could barely provide even for their families. The unsettling political and economic times had made an impact even within the enclosure of a holy abbey. Things would have to change.

The immediate problem that Eulalia noticed and mentioned to Cecilia was that the Saxons were quite lacking the normal daily discipline of proper members of the Benedictine Order, such as is found in

Normandy. The first day the Abbess entered the cloister while the Sisters were engaged in reading or writing, the Saxons remained as if they had not seen her. Only the Norman nuns stood, as was their duty. "Eh-hem!" she cleared her throat loudly, which drew the attention of all to her presence, and they got to their feet until she passed.

The practice of incensing the Abbess and Prioress by the priest at Vespers and Lauds was introduced as was the insistence on any Sister kneeling when sent a command by the Abbess, or in her absence, the Prioress. When anyone gives or receives anything from the hand of the Abbess, she shall kiss her hand, and if a Sister wishes to approach or depart from the Abbess she shall not do so before being so bid and saying Benedicite and bowing low. These disciplines are considered normal in Norman religious houses, but Saxon ones had become very lax.

"Just look at these habits!" Eulalia remarked to Cecilia as she scanned the Saxons. "There is hardly one that is properly black — look, that one has silver thread running through the hems, and that one is patterned most unfittingly! You must have words with Sister Lewina and insist upon the true Benedictine habits for all. Of course, the Vowesses and Lay Guests can wear what they like, but still, they should not flaunt their wealth by fine cloth and ornaments. While here in a religious house, they must conform to a suitable show of poverty and humility. If they do not like it, they are free to go!"

Such reprehensible carelessness of apparel was reflected in the liturgies too. The native nuns prayed in their own tongue, and they read from Scriptures translated into English, quite unlike the Continental usage where all is in Latin. King Alfred had apparently authorised this, by translating first the psalms and then other biblical books, and presenting them to the religious houses in his kingdom. It was well that Eulalia had been presented with Latin Scriptures, Sacramentaries and Lectionaries to bring with her. They replaced the older English ones.

As soon as she could, Abbess Eulalia insisted on Latin alone being used throughout. If the Saxons could not understand it, they would have to learn, and quickly. Provision was made for further language lessons for the Saxons. Sir Bertin would teach liturgical Latin to them as well as Norman French. If they could not understand their lessons or follow the readings in Latin, they could at least repeat the Ave, whose simple Latin even children could be taught.

(*'Ave Maria, gratia plena, Dominus tecum. Benedicta tu in milieribus, et Benedictus fructrus ventris tuae, Iesus.'* Luke 1:28,42).

Compared with the strict adherence to the Rule of St Benedict of Nursia followed in the great abbeys throughout the Continent, the Saxons were barely breathing the same air.

Between Shaftesbury Abbey's foundation, two hundred years ago, and now, discipline and the proper adherence to the Rule had been allowed to wax and wane, according to economic circumstances and to the character of the individual abbesses. About a century ago, one abbess, Herelufu adopted the reforms inspired by St Dunstan, Abbot of Glastonbury and who later became Archbishop of Canterbury. This increased numbers of men and women into the religious life and their sanctity — in equal measure. The two go together, there is no doubt.

These reforms revisited the sixth-century Rule and brought the Saxon liturgies into line with those on the Continent. Receiving the Eucharist every day and regularising the hours of prayer — including intercessions for the Saxon royal family — were then established.

But even the strictest reforms can peter out and be neglected under poor leadership and political uncertainty. Eulalia and Cecilia began studying together the great reforming document *Regularis Concordia*, composed by the Saxon Church leaders, Aethelwold and Dunstan, under King Edgar and approved by the Church Council of Winchester in AD

973. They had hoped that such a work would be known by the Saxon nuns, but when they mentioned it to them, were met by stony faces and glazed expressions. To implement it, so reckoned Eulalia, the two of them would first have to study it in detail.

Eulalia: A royal visitor, Queen Edith

I have asked Bishop Herman of Sherborne for a date for my installation as abbess. In fact I have asked several times. He is a learned but very disagreeable man. Whenever I send word to him he gives the impression that he had better things to do than listen to a woman! Anyway, I have now managed to obtain a date in June, appropriately on the feast of Saint Ethelreda, the Saxon foundress of a great dual abbey in Ely in the East of England. I shall send reminders of it until it happens.

Being Abbess-elect of a great royal abbey and pilgrimage centre which is situated between several other influential abbeys, as well as many lesser ones, means that I would host a number of important visitors during my time.

The first notable guest I was obliged to receive was the elderly Queen Edith, widow of King Edward the Confessor.

She came here from Wilton Abbey which has been her home since the Conquest, and where she was brought up as a child. She has suffered, I admit, having lost four brothers in just the one year, 1066 (three in one battle). She said that she was calling to pay her respects, but I suspect it was to look me over and see how her fellow Saxons were accepting us. She is a frail but haughty woman in her mid-fifties, and her great erudition is apparent from her speech — she is fluent in our form of the Frankish tongue as well as many other languages.

I was at a loss as to how to receive her. As sister to the late Harold Godwinson (or King Harold the Second, as the Saxons claim), she must be considered an enemy. But as crowned Queen she is entitled to respect, especially as a devout Christian, having rebuilt Wilton Abbey's wooden church with one of stone. Her immense wealth and former political influence have made her dominating and distant in her manner. Really, quite a difficult guest — not someone to whom I can warm. I learnt that her husband, King Edward had tried to divorce her back in 1051, and sent her away to live at the poor nunnery at Wherwell, but that her powerful family saw that she was reinstated. She made the most of that, forever after pulling the strings behind the throne, I hear.

We provided a feast upon her arrival, which she merely picked at, and she joined in with all our times of prayer. She told us she intends to travel to Winchester where she hopes to find better remedies for her health conditions than at

Wilton. That made me more than ever convinced that we must develop our cultivation of herbs and learn about the latest medicines and surgical procedures. It would be so good if this abbey could once again claim a reputation for the healing arts. After all, did not King Cnut come to us in his final days seeking a cure or at least a comfort in his dying? With all the abbeys and monasteries round about, for people of substance and influence to have to go for healing so far as Winchester is a disgrace.

After dinner on the second night of her visit, Queen Edith shared stories about other abbeys. It seems she has ways of knowing everything. I think she told us these accounts to make me uncomfortable. Mainly they were about the Norman monk from Fécamp, Turold, who was appointed Abbot of Malmesbury in 1067, but fell out with the community so badly that King William moved him to the abbey at Peterborough, saying that since Turold behaved more like a knight than an abbot, so that, "he might as well go where there was someone to fight" (William of Malmesbury). He arrived at Peterborough accompanied by a force of 160 fully armed knights. He must have expected trouble!

The Queen laughed at that, but I could not. She went on to tell me that the Peterborough monks had previously donated some relics of Saint Oswald to the Ramsey Abbey monks. Now Abbot Turold demanded them back, threatening to burn down their church if they did not comply. This Turold also fell out with Abbot Baldwin of

Bury St Edmunds because this good man refused to supply Turold with stone for his church-building project. It seems they argued and Turold was ordered to "get out and cause no more problems". Why did she tell me this? Abbots behaving badly and being sent away by kings and fellow abbots was not a subject of comfort to me in my new post.

I noticed that, even at prayer, her eyes were darting everywhere, assessing everything. She spoke with some of my Saxon nuns, who appeared awed and honoured to be addressed by such a person. Some simpered and giggled, which vexed me. When with us Normans, she frowned often and laughed little, belittling by insincere praise. I thought her most unpleasant.

The Queen left last Thursday after three nights, to my great relief, and I was delighted to receive Hugh of St Malo on the following day. He was passing through Shaftesbury on his way to Glastonbury Abbey, and had time just to change horses and have a small meal with me.

"Do not allow the old Queen to dismay you," he said, most charitably after I had relayed the tale of Turold. "But that is not the whole story. When on his way to claim the Peterborough abbey, a few years ago now, he arrived to find that the outlaw Hereward, known as the Vigilant, or the Wake, and his gang of Saxon rebels had plundered the abbey, setting both town and abbey alight. Only the church survived the flames."

"I had heard of this on the night of my arrival..." But Sir

Hugh was too excited by the story to hear my reluctance to hear it repeated. He just continued, with blazing eyes,

"With barefaced cheek, this devilish Hereward claimed he was simply safeguarding the treasure he plundered, which he took back to their centre at Ely! What is worse is that they captured and took several monks as hostages. He was in cahoots with Danes, can you believe? Anyone to fight us Normans and thwart us. The Danes took the treasure, and lost most of it when their fleet sank with it on board. They did save some of it, then that was destroyed in a fire in Denmark. God's work, obviously — not letting our enemies benefit from wicked acts against us. Anyway, you see why Abbot Turold needed to be so armed!"

I could indeed, but told him that really I prefer not to hear of such doings of violence. They do nothing to raise our thoughts to holier levels. Sir Hugh apologised for disconcerting me, but I let it pass and asked for him to convey our greeting to the Abbot of Glastonbury.

PART TWO
THE CONSECRATION OF THE ABBESS

Chronicle: The Eve, June 22, 1074

(This section is provided by Robert, Chaplain to Bishop Herman, and later to Abbess Eulalia: a friend of us at Shaftesbury)

Before the Conquest, Herman, Bishop of Sherborne, was the Chaplain to King Edward the Confessor and had been rewarded with the bishoprics of Ramsbury and Sherborne, both of which he kept at the same time — known as 'simony' and causing scandal.

Like our Queen Matilda, he is a native of Lotharingia (Flanders). But being neither Saxon nor Norman, he considers himself superior to both.

Summoned by Archbishop Lanfranc to an important reforming Church Council in London that Autumn, he felt he had to deal with the installation of the Abbess of Shaftesbury before that time. Maybe the friendship between our Abbess-elect and the Archbishop was the spur to this.

The night before the installation Bishop Herman hosted a feast for his ecclesiastics, abbots and priors from religious houses in the region, who were to stay in his palace for the event on the following day.

During the dinner, Glastonbury's dour Saxon Abbot Æthelnoth had attempted to regale the company with the details of all that he did, saw and said when King William took him with him to Normandy. A year after the Conquest the King obliged Abbot Æthelnoth, along with several other Saxon nobles of whose loyalty he had been unsure, to Normandy where he could keep them under surveillance. The Abbot moaned about how he had subsequently spent some miserable time held captive at Christ Church. There he had nothing to do but improve his Latin, before returning to Glastonbury. The company, those still listening, felt unsure how to receive this account, as any criticism of King William, overt or implied, could rebound unpleasantly on all concerned. An uncomfortable silence followed, and Æthelnoth regretted having spoken.

However, the mood lightened considerably after

the meal when Herman brought out his finest cider and invited his most honoured guest, the Norman Abbot Warin of Malmesbury, to address the company.

Not that Herman was much given to honouring others, as he was a man who cherished grudges. One he particularly nurtured concerned the appointment of Warin's predecessor-but-one, Beorhtric — happily, for Herman, deposed by King William shortly after his arrival in England. To honour Warin was to disparage Beorhtric.

Beorhtic's wrongdoing in Herman's eyes had been committed when he was Prior of the great royal Abbey of Malmesbury, centre of scholarship and influence, and Herman was only the Bishop of Ramsbury, Wiltshire, a minor See. Herman was determined to take on the Abbacy of Malmesbury himself when the position had become available and to transfer the bishopric there. As the trusted adviser at the time to King Edward, Bishop Herman secured the royal assent to the move, and looked forward to a grander style than he was afforded in Ramsey.

However, led by Prior Beorhtric, the monks of Malmesbury so opposed the plan, and enlisted the support of Earl Godwin and his son Harold (yes, that one, the claimant to the throne, defeated at Hastings), that after three days King Edward changed his mind and forbade it. Beorhtric became Abbot himself. Herman had been inflamed with fury, and leaving

Ramsbury in the care of another bishop, left England altogether. He became a monk at the Norman Abbey of Saint-Bertin. There he met the talented monk Goscelin, who joined him later in Wessex and wrote wonderful accounts of the sainted nuns at Wilton and elsewhere.

Three years later, when the bishopric of wealthy Sherborne became vacant, Herman applied for it and no one opposed him. So he returned and administered both that diocese and the one at Ramsbury, evicting the temporary bishop there.

Meanwhile Beorhtric was exiled by King William to the pitifully small and poor Benedictine Abbey of Burton in Staffordshire to make way for a Norman, Turold, a monk of Fécamp, to be appointed by King William as Abbot of Malmesbury.

That should have been that. But, as Queen Edith had recently related on her visit, Turold was extremely quarrelsome and argued so excessively with his community, that the king sent him to the far-away abbey of Peterborough. Reports from there circulated that he found opportunities to enrich himself prodigiously. It was at this time that Warin became Abbot of Malmesbury.

Warin amused his listeners with tales of monks of his abbey, particularly that of Eilmar, the "flying monk". Some years before, this young scholar of mathematics and astrology convinced himself that, with the right attachments to his arms and legs of 'sails', he could fly through the air. So equipped, he flung himself from a high tower and glided over the valley below for a considerable number of yards, until a sudden gust blew him back against the steep hillside and he suffered a broken leg.

"He felt sure," explained the present Abbot, "that with a proper rudder or tail-like attachment like a bird, he could have steered himself properly and avoided crashing."

The young monk was forbidden from attempting further flights and spent his considerably long life in writing and studying.

"He is still alive," Warin told his audience, "and wishes he were young again to make further attempts at sky-travel."

"Like Icarus — and look what happened to him!" called out one voice, met with hearty laughter. Warin should have left matters at that, but now in his cups began to tell how he had tossed out the bones of his predecessor Saxon saints from the abbey church into a far-off churchyard — all but for Saint Aldhelm's, which single one he held in respect. Not everyone present was comfortable with this, and wished he and his host had not entered into a drinking contest as he could not control his tongue when inebriated.

Herman's contribution, apart from the food and drink, was in declaring his avowed intention of moving the seats both of Sherborne and Ramsbury, neither supplying high enough incomes to sustain him as he would wish, to the ancient hill-fort of Sarum (Salisbury) — nearer to the political centre of Winchester and with excellent defences. He hoped the idea would be ratified by the forthcoming Council in London [It was].

"Ever since I came to this country from my home in Flanders I have found myself in situations, not of my making or choosing, of poverty."

There was some clearing of throats and many wry smiles as the diners looked around at the debris of an extravagant and delicious feast.

"Much is expected of someone in my position but, tell me, are those who expect it prepared to make sufficient contributions? Indeed not. You English, you Saxons or those of you of a Norman background, you do not realise how difficult it is for hardworking foreigners to make a decent living here! I came with no lands, no serfs, no titles — and have depended on my talents and the charity of others to see to my humble needs. Yet I do not grumble, no! I see what could be done and take steps to achieve it. And yet, I have so little time for myself. Why, just tomorrow I have to see to the installation of the new Abbess of Shaftesbury. Now that is an abbey worth ruling. Since King Alfred founded it almost two hundred years ago, it has received lands and wealth aplenty. Yet it is governed by a woman!"

A ripple of appreciative laughter met that, with much head-shaking and quiet comments that for women to possess such wealth and power was unnatural and possibly sinful.

Chronicle: The Day of the Consecration of Abbess Eulalia, June 23, 1074

On the day of the consecration Bishop Herman awoke with a hammering headache. He sent for his servant to fetch him some weak ale before helping him to dress.

"Damn Frankish wine," he muttered, forgetting that following the meal he had also swallowed numerous goblets of Normandy cider with the visiting Abbot Warin of Malmesbury and Abbot Æthelnoth of Glastonbury. The eve of the installation was for the gathering of churchmen. The day itself would include other dignitaries, secular and ecclesiastic.

The day itself was hot, good hunting weather, and the Bishop begrudged spending it on behalf of the Abbess of Shaftesbury. At least the wretched woman would stop pestering him for the date once the event was over.

Memories of the evening before began to clear in

Herman's mind, despite the unrelenting thudding of his head. Perhaps he and the Abbots of Glastonbury and Malmesbury should not have indulged in the drinking competition with quite so much abandon. He could not remember which of the three first fell under the table but was sure it was not him.

Now dressed, Herman prepared to receive the distinguished visitors from Shaftesbury. He was not in a cheerful mood, his head hurt, and his servant knew better than to chatter.

Dame Eulalia with her small group of Obedientes and Chaplain had stayed overnight in a small village her abbey owned, Abbas Combe, on the way between Shaftesbury and Sherborne. The building in stone of the Manor House was not finished, so their lodgings in the thatched wooden Great Hall were humble and uncomfortable, but as they spent the night largely in prayer and fasting, it mattered little.

Bishop Odo of Bayeaux, who owned the nearby village, had sent his blessing on beautifully inscribed vellum, which their tenant Aelfric presented to Eulalia with the greatest attitude of reverence.

Eulalia

The ceremony in the cathedral at Sherborne was conducted with due solemnity. There were readings from Scripture, particularly those showing Moses' sister Miriam as a model for abbesses. There was chanting of psalms and reciting of prayers. Extracts from the Rule of St Benedict were read out and a copy of the Rule presented to me. Much of the Ordo was from the Pontifical compiled in the previous century in St Alban's Abbey, Mainz, and some was unfamiliar to me, despite my having attended two previous consecrations. The ritual was similar to the consecration of an abbot, but the Latin male word endings were changed to female ones. It should, in my experience, have been also similar to that of a bishop in many respects. However, and here I was distressed to find that not only was the authority of my new office restricted to my "community" and not to the Church as a whole, but I was deprived of the presentation of a ring and a staff of office. Was I not the equal of a bishop, who would receive these symbolic objects? Am I to be subordinate? This was never the case before.

I later bought a ring and staff from Bishop Herman's Chaplain before I left, as I did not want my Sisters to see me without these ancient symbols of office. My seal shall depict me with them, I shall make sure of that.

There was much emphasis in the ceremony on women's chastity and virginity — something omitted in the ones for men. I am, according to this a "servant from the weaker sex" and the Bishop called upon God to send upon me the seven gifts of the Spirit as I need so much heavenly help in order to be worthy. I am to lead by the example of my chastity in order to present myself and my Sisters untainted to God. So it went on, until even I wearied of all the singing and praying and listening to Bishop Herman — whose Latin was not of the purest. The congregation, standing all the while, had become fidgety and began to chat among themselves. I hardly blamed them.

Chronicle: The After-Service Feast

The evening after the great event, and in accordance with custom, the new Abbess paid for a dinner in the Bishop's Palace, hosted by Bishop Herman, to which were invited all those illustrious civic and ecclesiastical guests who had attended her installation. One guest, a close friend of the Bishop from the Abbey of Saint-Bertin at Saint-Omer, was the quiet Benedictine writer, Goscelin (mentioned before).

Dame Eulalia had read works by him, mainly Lives of certain saints, and had been greatly impressed. She was delighted to have him introduced to her and determined to meet him again. He and Sister Cecilia sat beside each other and engaged in a long quiet discussion.

There were no fewer than four tables, like teeth in a comb, at right angles to the high, or top, table at whose centre sat the new Abbess and the Bishop. Close to that prestigious place, sat Walter, the Prior from Abbotsbury Abbey. He was obviously a cultured man, although wore a look of not caring much for the smell of those about him. He stood to intone the grace and added a blessing brought from his Abbot upon the distinguished newly-installed Abbess.

During the meal, he waved to attract Dame Eulalia's attention. Projecting his voice over the general hubbub, he asked if she had heard of the trouble that her friend Archbishop Lanfranc was having?

"No," she replied warily. She did not trust the glint in his eyes. There was a strong smugness in them over something. Why report a friend's problems, and with a smile?

"As you know," he related, "Lanfranc was to install Thomas of Bayeux as Archbishop of York, but demanded he swore an oath to obey him. York obey Canterbury! That he wouldn't do! The two, York in the North and Canterbury in the South, have been considered equals in all previous times, so why should he?"

"What happened?"

"They took the matter to His Holiness the Pope in

Rome who sided with Lanfranc. I tell you, the northern bishops aren't happy with that!"

Just then, Bishop Herman cut across the monk's laugh of triumph. "I think that's enough, Prior Walter. Don't upset our guest anymore."

"No, of course not!" declared the Prior with a deep intake of breath. Then, before anyone could stop him, he threw in, "But what does our guest know about our new King being denounced by Rome?"

"By Rome?" Eulalia could not suppress her anguish. She shushed her host and gestured to the Saxon Prior to explain himself immediately. He did so with relish.

"I hear that Pope Gregory is furious that the English bishops sacramentally anointed Duke William at his coronation. The meaning of anointing a man with oil is to ordain him a priest. The king is a layman so cannot be an ordained priest."

A general hubbub ensued.

"The Pope says that the bishops of the Church in England do not have the right to consecrate each other.."

"Disgraceful!"

"Rome is getting too powerful!"...

Similar sentiments were being shouted out from various parts of the hall, to Abbess Eulalia's amazement and horror.

"Nor can bishops preside over a coronation without

the express approval of the Bishop of Rome," contributed the Prior, relishing the consternation he was provoking.

This led to heated shouting between clerical and lay guests on the rights of the Church to interfere in those of the Kingdom, and vice versa. The Bishop-host tried to reclaim order.

"Brother, desist! This is an old case. Gregory the Seventh was not Pope when William was crowned. The present Pope has many other concerns!"

"Like priestly celibacy! He is violently opposed to priests being married," shouted out one disgruntled voice.

"They say he is producing an encyclical denying the authority of bishops who ordain married priests, and saying that lay people need not obey such bishops!"

"Terrible!"...

"Such interference"...

"New ideas undermining old customs."

"They say he also opposes holding more than one diocese or benefice at the same time!"

"Then bishops will starve!"

That brought on some laughter, mainly from the laity present.

"They say the Emperor Henry the Fourth is considering appointing his own pope."

"Yes, I heard that — Clement, I believe..."

By now Bishop Herman had to shout loudly to

restore order, banging his knife upon the table to be heard over the hubbub.

"Please, let us hear more from Abbotsbury's Prior. Facts, please; not opinions. Sir Walter, continue."

"You are correct about the encyclical. I myself am on my way to Rome to help Pope Gregory publish it, called Dictatus Papae I understand, that will confirm that only the Pope can appoint and depose bishops, kings and rulers, and that all secular kings and rulers must owe him fealty and obey him in all matters. Then King William will see that he cannot order about the Church in this land — appointing bishops and abbots as he wills!"

Eulalia by now felt weak and tearful at this treasonable diatribe against her esteemed King. She was a loyal Norman — a friend of the Queen indeed. Had not the King himself appointed her at Shaftesbury? But she also belonged to the Church, owing obedience to the Pope, the legitimate head of it, successor of the Apostle Peter.

She had never heard of such confusing and contradictory claims, and her head spun. As her loyalties were stretched in both directions, the food she had just consumed rose to her throat to make her nauseous.

Some of her associates sitting close to her noticed her discomfort. One of her guests from Shaftesbury, Sheriff Fitzgrip, was on his feet, shouting at the

Abbotsbury monk to be silent and ordering him to leave the hall. His wife tugged at his sleeve in alarm and shook her head when he glanced at her. Quickly moderating his tone, he bade the monk say his *post cibum Benedictus* at once and then depart. The whole assembly rose to its feet for him to intone the Latin grace, adding a loud Amen. Then the Prior took his leave through the hall.

Once he had gone, the subdued chatter confirmed the general disapproval both of the monk's cruel treatment of the lady guest of honour, the new Abbess, and of his message concerning their Church and their King. For an English king to submit to a foreign power far away was unheard of and outrageous interference. Tradition meant everything, and the Faith of the Christian Church in England, nurtured and flourishing despite heathen attacks and invasions for over a millennium, was too precious to cede to outsiders. Such were their views, expressed quietly now, but forcefully. King William himself understood this and continued to encourage devotions to certain Saxon and Celtic saints, particularly royal ones, such as those at Shaftesbury. Queen Matilda had a great devotion to Saint Cuthbert, which was shrewd of her and helped to quell the rebelliousness of their northern subjects. There had been no division between Church and State for a Millennium, and English bishops had confirmed the legitimacy of kings, looking back over history, not over sea and land to Rome.

The guests then turned to the array of fine food before them. Venison, swan, rabbit and pork was plentiful, root vegetables and cheeses abounded and there were great heaps of bread left largely untouched. Wine and Normandy cider were being quaffed by all present, some to the point of near-inebriation. When most of the piles of food and joints of meat had been demolished, happier chatter, laughter and the attempts at singing and reciting verse, commenced.

Eulalia: **Returning to Shaftesbury, and the Beginning of Horror**

On our return to Shaftesbury Abbey, bringing with us Sir Robert, Bishop Herman's Chaplain and representative, we were met at the great gateway on Bimport with a satisfyingly solemn procession of all the Sisters. Just inside the enclosure I prostrated myself fully, secretly thanking God the ground was dry. The Sisters began their chant as we processed to the chapel where I underwent the second prostration, facing the altar. Sir Robert, taking the place of the bishop, at the end of the chant, led me to my elaborately carved seat of office to the right of the altar. While the Te Deum was being sung each nun, Norman and Saxon, came up in turn to offer me the kiss of peace, genuflecting before and after the kiss. I wondered just what the Saxons were thinking as they did that, and prayed that none would do or say anything unseemly. Sir Robert and Sir Bertin then said a Mass after which we processed to the chapter-house.

There I confirmed all the offices and duties that had been temporarily laid upon the Obedientes and others, and we proceeded then to a festive meal in the refectory, at which Sir Robert and I were the central figures. I was pleased and proud that the Sisters had performed all the ceremony and the standings and genuflections called for with a discipline of which I would not have imagined them capable just a few months before. I felt that Archbishop Lanfranc would have approved, and somehow, that mattered a lot.

After Sir Robert left, waving farewell from the gateway to the enclosure, taking good impressions to relay to Bishop Herman, I returned alone to my house to rest.

Then began a series of frightful happenings.

The first was the sight of a dead crow upon the threshold of my house. Such a thing is most unnatural, as most creatures tend to find quiet secluded places in which to die. I went to the abbey kitchen, where I usually can find her, and called Margot to come at once. She was clearly frightened by the sight, slapping her hands to her mouth.

"My Lady Abbess," she cried out, "This is a sign from the devil! It means death! Heaven and all the saints help us!" I believe she would have fallen in a faint had I not shaken her and chided:

"Nonsense, woman, it did not get here by itself or by the Devil's hand, although the Devil has entered somebody's heart, someone here. They want to frighten us. They'll be really happy if they hear you scream out like that!"

That was just the first of several nocturnal 'gifts' upon my doorstep over the following weeks. On other mornings we found a dead rat, a headless cat, a disembowelled kitten and a toad impaled on a sharp stick, and sometimes large drops of blood. Someone within the enclosure obviously wanted to finish what the poisoner began. The thought that we harboured someone of such ill-will frightened me, especially as the animosity seemed to be directed towards me rather than anyone else, but I did not fear, as poor Margot did, the poor dead creatures as satanic. They were used simply and cruelly as human threats.

Each night as I lay to sleep I paraded the Saxons before me in my mind to see who among them would poison us and who would want to scare me away. Were they the same person? Were there more than one? What if the majority of nuns wanted us gone so much they would kill us or frighten us out of our wits? — for poor Margot was becoming more and more beside herself each morning when she found the 'things'. I too felt sick to the stomach, but could not let my servant see that weakness, or she would have collapsed altogether.

While I lay there in the dark, listening to Margot's snores, owls hooting and foxes bark, I listened out for footsteps so that I could run out and find whoever it was leaving the deathly 'gifts'. Sometimes I thought I heard the sound of human footfall, but in the stillness realised it was simply the hooves of horses in the nearby stables, or the trotters of pigs in their styes. Some people did have legitimate reasons to walk about — checking on the hens and geese, or tending to a sick or calving cow.

Servants were up and about before dawn, lighting fires and collecting water left at the side gate in pitchers brought up on New Forest ponies from the springs and ponds at the foot of the hill. The water from the northern hamlet of Enmore Green, which lay immediately below the town, was needed to supplement the well and cistern water collected within the enclosure. It was such good spring water, we could almost drink it as it was, without fermenting it as beer or mixing it with wine. The animals needed great quantities of it, of course. We used it for washing our hands and faces, and for cleaning the buildings. Laundry was cleaned using water below the southern slope, where there are also springs, but not of such good quality.

Anyway, one night, I lay in bed praying inwardly and intently listening. I heard a twig break nearby, just beyond the wooden wall of my simple house. I fancied I could hear deep breathing too, whereas Margot's snores were different. I froze and held my breath until I nearly fainted. Definitely there was a step taken here and another there. Someone was right up to the house wall and making for the entrance. I quickly promised myself to build a sturdy stone lodging with locks and keys as a priority, even if the church building had to be delayed. These wooden Saxon homes were inadequate for safety. While I slept on the ground floor in the inner room, Margot, deep asleep, lay between the entrance door and me. I knew she would not be able to withstand an armed intruder. I was right.

The plank placed as a fastener across the door on the inside was slowly being lifted on one side. I could not see, but could hear it slowly edging upwards to the top of the holding bracket until it fell out quietly. Then the same action took place through the slit between door and frame at the other end, where the hinges are. Someone was using something to lift the plank clear of both brackets until it fell clear with such a thud on the floor that the noise awakened Margot. She and I both shot up from our beds and shouted out "Help! Help!" as the door opened showing, in silhouette against the moonlight, a tall cloaked figure.

I grasped the pewter candlestick from the little table beside the bed, and so armed, ran forward to see, barely in the gloom, the form of a person with hand upraised, holding a long knife, blade down, gleaming with reflected moonlight. With a blood-chilling yell of fury this intruder brought down the weapon onto the body of my poor Margot, who screamed loud and fell backwards, suddenly silent. At once, the attacker turned to me, raising again the knife to strike it upon me, and yelling something in the Saxon tongue I did not understand. But I knew the intention. As the knife was launched towards me I swung the candlestick. Providentionally it caught the blade with great force. With the clash of metal on metal, the weapon was wrenched from the would-be assassin's hand. Frustrated and maddened further, the woman, for it was a woman's voice, stretched out her hands towards my neck and almost fell upon me.

I grabbed her arms and with a strength I did not know I could muster, kept them from allowing her hands from fully encircling my throat. Her fingertips dug into my neck and I could feel spittle from her mouth as she continued to yell into my face. The force of her weight pushed us both back into my room and towards the bed. I feared being thrown backwards onto it as in that low position I would be deprived of the strength to withstand being strangled.

As the attacker pushed, I resisted, wondering how long I would be able to so do, and totally unable to overcome her. Was this when I would meet my death, so shortly after my installation as abbess here? In my head I sent up my most fervent prayer for deliverance, while, with vile ear-splitting shouting, her bitter breath assaulted my face.

Margot, recovering from the shock of her attack, and bleeding from a deep shoulder wound, had the wit to pick up the piss-pot from under the end of my bed, lifted it high and brought it down upon the head of the assailant. Fortunately it was empty!

With a yell of surprise, the woman released her attempt on my throat and turned towards Margot. I leapt to the side of her and, before she knew what was happening, picked up the bedside table itself and brought it down heavily upon her. This time she fell, not quite unconscious, but stunned.

By the light of the moon I saw the knife blade glinting on the floor some feet away. I picked up the weapon to turn it upon the perpetrator if needed. Meanwhile Margot, too excited to feel the pain of her wound yet, had the presence of mind to sit upon the woman — and her weight is not inconsiderable!

Thus disabled, the Saxon assailant lay, swearing and cursing — or so it sounded — until help arrived. Sir Bertin had heard our shouts for help, and the wild screaming of the miscreant, and had hurried as fast as he was able. Behind him from a further distance came the two gatekeepers, younger, fitter men, and other workmen from their houses alongside the enclosure wall which ran alongside Bimport. They soon took custody of the attacker, who once she was outside, we could see was Lady Goldiva, the wealthy laywoman I had long distrusted. "Lock her up," I commanded, "but do no harm to her!"

Sir Bertin and I accompanied poor shaking Margot to the infirmary to have her wound attended. Thanks to Saints Elfgivu and Edward, whose intercession I invoked, she made a full recovery.

I considered what to do with the Lady Goldiva. To report her crime to Sheriff Fitzgrip would ensure her death and possibly that of her closest associates — but that could turn the Saxon community in town and abbey against us all. I could not risk that. Besides, the woman was raving, out of her mind — no doubt possessed by demons. Sir Bertin and I placed her in the custody of her sister and brother-in-law, who live in a Manor House not ten miles away. They undertook to obtain the services of an exorcist, and in any case, to keep her in close confinement. She had lost her father in battle, and her small two sons, who had perished from sickness after being confined in a damp dark dungeon with other Saxons while their father was being hunted as a dangerous rebel. He had been caught and killed too and his head presented to her as a cruel "gift". All these had affected her mind and even the ministrations of the gentle nuns at Shaftesbury could not heal her.

When I heard her story, I felt I had done the right thing in sparing her life. Who could withstand such hardships? I asked for prayers for her from all the nuns and, apart from Margot who could never forgive her, that seemed to please our Saxon Sisters. I felt the relationship between our two peoples had begun to improve.

Although, with Goldiva constantly denying that she taken any part in the poisoning a few months previously, that still left someone, or more than one, Saxon living among us who had wished us very ill and may still do. I tried not to let that fear obsess me, although I habitually observe each of them closely for any signs of malevolence in their nature.

PART THREE
THE STORY CONTINUES

Chronicle: 1074-1086

So began the early years under Abbess Eulalia when the Abbey of St Mary and St Edward began to be turned into a zealous and observant Benedictine community.

But to flourish, the abbey needs to raise a church worthy of it. That became a high priority, to build on the massive scale for which Normans are reknowned. The very first wooden chapel, roofed with wooden tiles rather than thatch, was built when King Alfred's daughter became Abbess. Small and dark, it was soon replaced in a more southerly spot by a larger stone building, the one in use when we first arrived. Abbess Eulalia had that larger one demolished to prepare for her greater, much more magnificent new church. The original one was re-opened as a church to serve then as our chapel until enough of the new church's chancel was constructed for us to use.

Then, after we moved into the new chancel and transepts, the original one, dedicated to the Holy Trinity, was presented to the townspeople for their uses. That too was rebuilt in stone over time as were many more churches, built to accommodate all the many pilgrims streaming to the martyred Saint King Edward's shrine.

There was so much building both within the enclosure, of a new cloister and houses, and in the town, rebuilding those homes destroyed after the expulsion of the former Abbess Leveva, that sometimes the noise and dust were quite overpowering. We forbade the masons and builders from shouting to each other, so they developed a complex system of hand signs instead — as we have during silent meals in the refectory, when we listen to readings and need something to be passed from our neighbour. Our silent sign language is more subtle, of course.

Part of the Abbess's plans for developing the Abbey at Shaftesbury, was to encourage the devout, both clergy and lay, rich and poor, from all over the world, to attend the shrines of the royal saints. Pilgrims would find healing of body and mind by praying in proximity to the relics, as their heavenly influence would be greater in that place than in any other. It is as if heaven and earth were brought together.

Miracles occurred, some of which we knew (and for which we gave thanks) but others would only be known over time and when the pilgrims had returned home. What is sure is that merit would be applied to the devout pilgrim for having accomplished a holy pilgrimage, perhaps in honour of a vow taken, or for healing or on behalf of a loved one who has died. Such merit gained and recorded in heaven would benefit the pilgrim on their death or be transferred to another already dead. That is when the length and degree of necessary suffering in Purgatory would be decided in the Heavenly Court. For who does not want to reduce the time in that fiery place when heaven itself stands ready, with all the angels and saints, to greet the soul once it has been purged and purified? Purgatory is a necessary place and time is needed for the process, for no soul tainted with unpardoned sin can enter the spotless place that is Eternal Bliss.

Eulalia: Archbishop Lanfranc's Visit, Spring 1079

Shortly after Cecilia and I began our studies of the reforms written in the last century, my dear friend Archbishop Lanfranc wrote to tell me of his intended visit shortly. As the days lengthened and the sun grew stronger I began to look forward to the visit my esteemed friend from Caen who is now, as Archbishop of Canterbury, the highest churchman in England. I still think of him as an abbot as he had been that of our 'brother' Abbey, St Stephen's, in Caen. I heard that it was he who suggested to Queen Matilda that a member of our Trinity Abbey should be appointed to this one in England. She spoke to her husband, King William, and so here I am! Dear Lanfranc said he was most gratified by my appointment — and the approval of such a man delights me.

It was through him that the two abbeys in Caen were originally built. Way back he had opposed the marriage of William of Normandy with Matilda of Flanders, on the grounds of consanguinity — they were third cousins once removed, and so fell within the rule of 'not within seven degrees of relatedness'. They went ahead and got married in defiance of him and of the Pope. As a form of penance, they founded these two abbeys in 1060 and were thereby reconciled with the Church and with Lanfranc. (Just as King William built an abbey at Battle near Hastings, as the Pope had deplored so much bloodshed, and just as King Alfred had built this abbey and one for men at Athelney in Somerset after his victory at Edington against the Vikings).

(Instruction — record all this to educate the future young novices who may not know how the twin great abbeys in Caen began).

Of course I had met him as Abbot when I was a novice

and newly professed nun, learning how to write and copy manuscripts and being instructed in what to read and learn. He was such an influence on me, as he is on all the monastic communities of Normandy and beyond.

The day came when I was privileged to welcome him here. He was escorted along Bimport by Steward Thibault and Sheriff Fitzgrip with their men. The joy of seeing him again after several years was immense. From his smiles I believe he felt the same! His kind face, with its long thin nose and high cheekbones, was looking older, but no less benign. After some refreshments, we easily fell into discussion — with Sir Bertin keeping a respectful distance just out of earshot, his presence protecting us from any hint of scandal. Sir Bertin was not an admirer of the great reformer, as Lanfranc insists that priests must be and remain celibate. Sir Bertin, having been married and loved his wife, felt that was too harsh. He had whispered to me once, in discussing Lanfranc's reforms,

"You can oblige a man to be celibate, but you cannot make him chaste!" Such a sentiment in a woman would be scandalous, but I understand that men are weaker in this regard. I admit to a feeling of discomfort with this harsh reform, as the married secular priests I have known seem to be kinder, more understanding of women than the single ones. The monks at Wareham certainly did not convince me that the absence of any female element in their lives was a good thing — they seemed so bitter and sad.

Anyway, my guest arrived and at once declared that he

was delighted about our plan for reforms here. Oh, that really thrilled me.

He went on, "As you know I achieved a degree of reform of our Benedictine Order in Normandy and elsewhere, but the English are so reluctant to change — especially when change comes from the mouth and pen of a Norman! (For although Lanfranc was born and raised in Italy, he has lived and worked so long in Normandy as to be considered a native of there now.)

He described the major teaching document he is working on, to be called 'The Monastic Constitutions', which should, if heeded, put an end to the widespread abuses within monastic communities and the shameful relaxation in many of them of the Rule of St Benedict. He spoke warmly about his protégé, Anselm, whom I knew slightly, the Prior (then Abbot) at the Abbey at Bec, Lanfranc's former monastery before he went to Caen. Another Italian, Anselm is a very distinguished man known throughout Europe as a great scholar. His influence, Lanfranc informed me, was growing everywhere daily, causing men and women in religious orders to engage in learning from the wisdom of the Fathers of the Church and even from the classical philosophers before them.

I then asked Archbishop Lanfranc about the trouble he himself was having with the theologian Berengarius, whose views I considered alarming. "You see," I said somewhat mischievously, "we do know what is going on in high places!

The affairs of Pope Gregory in Rome are known even in this remote spot!"

He agreed that Canon Berengarius' views are quite dangerously heretical, considering his scholarship affects so many in the Church, not just in the cathedral school at Tours, but even here the novices talk about them. But, he assures me, Pope Gregory is determined to obtain a confession from Berengarius of true faith in the doctrine of transubstantiation, of the Real Presence of Christ in the consecrated bread and wine at communion.

He confided in me that the Pope and he together had drawn up a document which the theologian would sign, on pain of excommunication. In this he would affirm that the bread and wine that are placed on the altar are 'through the mystery of the sacred prayer and the words of our Redeemer substantially changed into the true and proper life-giving flesh and blood of Jesus Christ our Lord; and that after the consecration they are the true body of Christ'. The Archbishop then reminded me of the old legend, concerning the first Pope Gregory. Apparently, during Mass, in response to a deacon scoffing at belief in the Real Presence, the crucified Lord Himself rose up behind the altar, and blood poured from his wounds, his stigmata, into the chalice held by the presiding priest, Pope Gregory.

"I should like to see that depicted," I said. "Maybe one day we could have a statue of that scene, in painted stone, in the new abbey church."

"That would be wonderful," he beamed, as we walked together.

After a while, finding talking more difficult when walking, we sat down on a low wall and he fetched me a letter from inside the folds of his habit. I unscrolled the parchment and was amazed at what I saw. "You are writing this to a bishop?" I exclaimed.

He nodded, with a conspiratorial smile.

"You see what I am up against?" he whispered as I read,

"Give over dice-playing, not to speak of even worse misconduct and worldly sports, in which you are said to waste the whole day. Study theology..." I could barely read more, struck between wanting to laugh out loud and feeling nausea that a senior churchman, the Bishop of Elmham no less, needed such a reproof. How brave was my friend to write in such straightforward tones.

"I have plans," added Lanfranc on taking the letter from me and hiding it again within his habit. "I am calling councils of senior churchmen together every couple of years to sort out abuses. You have no idea the resistance I find! All radical change needs strength to carry it through, and I draw mine both from God and from the support of my King. I shall see that no priest is married. Families drain the resources of the church and divide the loyalty of the men in charge of souls. I shall transfer cathedrals from where they are within small settlements into the new cities — for cities are the future. That is where the people are increasingly

beginning to gather together, for trade, markets and manufacturing, so we must be there for them."

He was now talking more quickly, with excitement, and my heart was beating faster knowing I was being privy to all these wonderful plans and reforms. This next caused me to hold my breath, its implications were so transformative.

"Finally," he said, with emphasis, "and this is possibly the most radical, I shall organise the secular clergy into single churches in every settlement. They shall be parishes, each with their own priest, as the centre in each community. Monasteries and great abbeys like this will, of course, always play their part, a vital part, but while people live remote from priests they are remote from the Word of God and the sacrament. Soon every peasant, every merchant, every man and woman, will have a church serving them — and God — in their own neighbourhood. And the priests will be educated to explain the Holy Scriptures to the people."

I was stunned again. This is breakthrough planning, changing the very structure of the Church in this land. What a man! What a leader!

It was a warm Spring day, with a cloudless sky and, quite unusually for the hilltop, no wind. So with Sir Bertin trailing behind, I showed my esteemed friend around the enclosure, the barns, stables and and dwellings of workers,

the dormitories of the sisters and the houses of the pensioners and Vowesses. He did not need to see the cellars and kitchen, but he inspected the chapter-house and the counting house next to the great gatehouse.

Knowing the efficacy of plants in the healing arts, he asked to look around the herbularius (for medicinal herbs) and spoke much in favour of it. He felt our general herb and vegetable gardens were not quite those of St Gall's (the model of monastic horticulture)! But they were well enough, especially as the tenanted lands around our hill were blessed with rich soil and plentiful plant life. He asked when the villeins upon these lands, and their serfs and cottagers, worked the days due to their lord, or in our case, lady. "Mondays and Fridays," I replied, although in fact these could change during the week if there were feasts on which they could not work. There are several children who are now coming to working age so that the next few harvests should be secure, for labour anyway — we cannot depend on weather and pestilence!

∼

Shortly after noon we watched together as, first the Norman Sisters and after a small gap, the Saxon ones filed out in pairs from saying the Office of Sext in Holy Trinity. We did not go with them for their meal, instead I told him the whole of my situation as a Norman here, with which he sympathised. He appreciated the difficulties in trying to govern where many of my Sisters and all of the lay men and women are Saxon and detest us heartily.

I showed him the hospital where Cnut, the great king of Denmark, Norway and England, died after a lengthy illness forty or so years ago. Unfortunately, his body is not buried here, but in Winchester. As we walked, he told me about his disgraceful Saxon predecessor at Canterbury, Stigand, Chaplain to Cnut and all the English kings since. That churchman had been bishop of the two richest dioceses, Winchester and Canterbury, at the same time and been excommunicated for it by the Popes in Rome no fewer than five times! His appointment to Canterbury was questionable, as he had received the pallium from the anti-reformist anti-Pope Benedict X, but yet it was unheard of to hold two wealthy dioceses together. He appointed his own brother to the bishopric of Elmham, which he had held previously, but also — although not a monk — controlled the Abbeys of Gloucester, Ely and others. Such scandal! Such corruption! I was astounded but reassured to hear that this Stigand had died in captivity in Winchester two years ago. He had been arrested and imprisoned there by the papal legates four years after the Conquest.

We then walked to the site of the demolished former abbey chapel which now boasts the foundations and parts of the walls for a magnificent round-arched, enormous church in the style of ones in Rome. The Archbishop admired the outline of the structure and the industry of the masons, Saxon and Norman labourers working together.

From there we went over to the Holy Trinity chapel, nearer Bimport, and to the shrines of the royal saint, King Edward. The relics had been removed from the abbey church before it was demolished and have been placed as a temporary measure in smaller adjacent structures in the nave near the west door in Holy Trinity. When we are not praying in there, pilgrims file in one way, through the west door, to touch or kiss the shrine and exit through the door in the north wall. They come, men and women alike, from all walks of life and some from incredible distances. They leave better, full of faith and hope. Lanfranc smiled broadly as he kissed the shrine and I inwardly rejoiced.

I promised him that I would send him a piece of a finger-bone of Saint Edward as a first-degree relic and a piece of his shroud as a second-degree one. He was very pleased and said that he would place both in beautifully worked reliquaries and put them on display in his cathedral. It will kindle much devotion in the hearts of all who see it as they learn of the martyr's story, and may be inspired to come here.

It was with great delight that I informed the Archbishop that I had commissioned the Flemish monk Goscelin, whom I had met at my installation, to write the "Passion of St Edward, King and Martyr". This work is nearing completion and the author tells me it exalts the many virtues of the saint and recounts some of the miracles obtained through his heavenly intercession. Archbishop Lanfranc at once promised to obtain a copy once it was finished and would send one of his own scribes to see to it. Such joy that gives me.

Unfortunately, the Archbishop was much less enthusiastic about the cult of the sainted Queen Aelfgifu. He explained that, while deploring the action of some Norman abbots and bishops in disparaging Saxon saints, he felt it was more worthwhile to concentrate on the cults of those who had made a substantial contribution to the spiritual life of the nation, and who presented with well-testified lives and miracles. King Edward was one such, but Aelfgifu much less so. We had no certifiable bones of the Queen, nothing of hers except a pestle and mortar that the saint used in grinding herbs to be used in healing, That is but a poor third-degree relic and one which is largely ignored here, simply placed in a box for safekeeping. Lanfranc suggested that it would be better put to use in the infirmary, as I am sure the saint would have wanted.

Before he left I walked with the Archbishop along the southern edge of the enclosure above our vineyard and orchard, to show him the views over the valleys. Distant wooded hills, pastures of sheep and fields full of golden wheat, all give a sense of God's bounty, and provide me with satisfaction, knowing that all the land we can see, and much beyond, belongs to us.

Leaving the enclosure to cross Bimport, we then followed a short path between trees, and came upon the northern edge of the hilltop. From there we could see across many miles of wooded valley to ranges of hills on the horizon. We could just make out the mighty Abbey of Glastonbury — an abbey that can rival ours for wealth and land. Because it is for men, it surpasses us in influence, for at times the abbot of that community has been appointed to a bishopric, even an archbishopric — an honour denied us because of our sex. There are some people in the Church who consider men's prayers are more efficacious than ours, because, I presume, they can offer Masses. That unfortunately for us leads them to receive more offerings and therefore income than we do.

Lanfranc shook his head.

"That is not right," he said. "Although many theologians and churchmen consider that women are the source and cause of sin, and therefore are not even fitted for heaven, there are those, like myself, who consider that the prayers of female virgins, like those of the Mother of Christ, reach to heaven before all else — even those of popes and kings."

Such a wise and understanding man. How blessed is England that he has power and influence within the nation.

I informed him that, with our High Steward and other functionaries, we will introduce a more efficient use of the land, on the Norman model, and that should help prevent the widespread failures of crops that the Saxons endured. Plus, once the rebels have been subdued throughout the land, the peace that we Normans will be able to bring should ensure prosperity.

He nodded in agreement.

While returning through the enclosure we came across

bushes of white broom, an unusual colour as the plant is normally bright yellow. I explained their presence to him, as I had been told, that they concerned a miracle involving the young Saint Edward. On the procession here with his murdered, martyred body from Wareham, where he had lain for a year, wherever his coffin was laid down for the bearers to rest, there sprang up bushes of white broom. So we grow it now to supply small sprigs of it to the pilgrims as tokens. Worn on their outer clothes it leads others to enquire the reason for it, and so spreads the word of our mission.

"Very wise," he remarked.

I mentioned Saint Aelfgifu to him again, in the hope that he would change his mind and affirm her significance. I told him that we had prayed to her on our perilous sea crossing, and that she was known around these parts for her good works in her lifetime. Her intercession had brought many acts of healing, I have been told by various people. I said that I felt we should rekindle interest in her, as the heavenly influence of a female saint housed in an all-women's abbey could be helpful to other women, troubled women. I said that her feast days were well-supported by the people in the town, and that they had a fondness for her.

Lanfranc asked when we held the feast day of St Aelfgifu here. I told him on May 18th and we also celebrated the anniversary (inventio) *on August 18th of the finding of her body here exactly one hundred years ago, though we are not sure where it is now. He told me that he believed that these feast days are also celebrated in many other great abbeys in this land, and admitted that that fact shows the importance of our St Aelfgifu and that, perhaps after all, devotion to her should be encouraged.*

Before the Conquest, because these royal saints attracted pilgrims from across the land, the town had grown to the east of the abbey, and the abbey's coffers were filled. The town too flourished and there were no fewer than three royal coining mints, which shows how flourishing and well regarded Shaftesbury was before the Conquest. Alas, the opposition to Norman rule and the consequent devastation wrought by our avenging troops has set the town back — I hope not fatally. Demolished houses can be rebuilt and prosperity return.

Sometimes failures in communities, religious or secular, lead to a spiral of decline until total collapse is inevitable. To prevent that happening here we must be vigorous in encouraging Shaftesbury to become once again a centre attracting hosts of pilgrims. After all, the donations they bring enhance our coffers and their payments for services and accommodation benefit the town's inhabitants. By these means we shall secure good relations between us and the Saxons. Archbishop Lanfranc agreed and said that he would help in our objectives by all the means he could. For example, he offered to recommend pilgrimages here as penances for grievous sins, or to seek out healings and cures for ailments.

I was so grateful to him, and so sad when he had to leave, but his duties are many.

DEBORAH M JONES

Chronicle

After that momentous visit from the foremost church leader in the land, life in the Abbey followed a regular pattern of prayer, work, study, meals and sleep. Manuscripts were copied and illustrated, children educated, the sick tended and the destitute relieved. Revenues were collected in coin or kind, and the spiritual life advanced with reading, prayer and meditation.

As summer progressed, tempers sometimes frayed with the heat, but were quickly calmed through the thoughtful intervention of the prioress or her deputy. At one time Abbess Eulalia herself had to intervene in a verbal dispute between a Saxon nun and a Norman one. She will not tell me their names, but apparently their argument was at risk of becoming violent, with one brandishing a serving spoon towards the head of the other. Loud voices, almost screaming at each other, are intolerable in a holy place, and the Abbess had to severely reprimand the two miscreants and, at the next Chapter meeting, obliged the two to confess their sin before the whole community and receive appropriate penance — which included having to sleep in the dormitory of the other and share meals at the table of the other's community.

The Abbess was usually able to leave discipline to

the Norman Prioress and her Saxon Assistant while she oversaw the bigger picture — checking the finances were well managed and the Rule of St Benedict followed closely in every detail. As the fifth-century Rule was written for men, and in the warm climate of Monte Cassino in southern Italy, she had to adapt it where necessary. Here in hill-top Shaftesbury a chilly wind can blow from any direction with nothing in its path to stop it. Rain can sweep across the summit and cascade down the steep slopes, and mist settle below on the valley floors, carpeting it until midday in thick white cloud with just the distant undulating ridges visible. Mainly, though, summer weather can be pleasantly hot while the winters bitterly cold. Extra layers and thicker cloth for habits were allowed and even the wearing of travelling trousers underneath the skirts permitted for the Sisters most vulnerable to seasonal colds.

The building projects advanced well, the wall rising higher and higher, although a few of the labourers fell from the scaffolds and were either killed or broke bones. The kindness of the Abbess saw that their widows and families received small pensions and were put to such work as they were able to accomplish.

Every year one or two Sisters died, either Saxon or Norman, from illness or old age. Occasionally a Sister or servant would suffer an accident, such as tripping over a stray lump of masonry left by a careless worker or being bitten by a snake while collecting apples or grapes growing on the southern slope. Sister Wynna, who cooked for the Saxons, was one who died of breathing sickness, and was replaced by a young Saxon, Hild. Known to be giddy and silly beforehand, from the hard work in the kitchen, with sensible servants, she became a steadier and more mature Religious Sister. Such improvements of character were always pleasing to the Abbess, who set great store on the value of common sense united with deep piety and serious study. Abbess Eulalia worried when any of her Sisters seemed not to be so devoted to spiritual improvement and community service as she should be, and often drew them into conversation in her quarters, the better to listen to their concerns and encourage their religious understanding. Her penances were always thoughtfully considered.

The death of some Sisters did not deplete the numbers of the community, as more came to join it almost monthly. Not long after the death of Sister Wynna, three young recruits arrived, two single women and a scarcely older widow, who all wished to enter our abbey. Of the two girls, one is of impeccable Norman noble ancestry, and seems an ideal candidate. The other, Astrid, is half Danish and half Saxon but brought up in a civilised household. When the last Dane to rule England, Harthacnut, came over to Sandwich in Kent in 1040, her father was a young warrior in his fleet of over sixty warships. He settled in Kent and married a Saxon, adopting her Christianity and sending his daughter Astrid to be raised by nuns. The girl had long expressed a desire to come to Shaftesbury Abbey as the great King Cnut had died here, and she held him in tremendous admiration. Oh well, time will tell if she progresses in the novitiate before the commitment of her full profession.

The widow, Marie de Soissons, had been bereaved by the natural death of her husband, a wealthy landowner and, having no children or male heirs, she was able to bring with her a generous dowry and two personal servants — humble, obliging women, whose services she donated to the community.

One late summer's day, with nature at its most fecund, another small party of Sisters with a number of servants, arrived accompanied by an armed guard, from the Abbey of the Trinity in Caen. With them came a consignment of cider and wine in a cart, a generous gift from its patron, Queen Matilda. The Abbess at Caen, another Matilda, had given the senior Sister, sub-Prioress Agnes, a letter for Abbess Eulalia in which she asked if she would agree to take a novice, Lady Hélène of Honfleur, into the community. The sub-Prioress, being a sensible and amiable young person, Eulalia warmed to at once, told how she had interviewed the parents of this girl, for she was hardly more than a child, and could tell that these high-born folk were not happy. It seemed that young Hélène was insisting on entering religious life, but whether it was simply more to avoid marriage with Sir Arsène of Sourdeval than to engage in a lifetime of prayer and discipline, no one knew. Sir Arsène is wealthy and well regarded by King William, but admittedly he is more than twenty-five years older than the girl, of vaster build, drinks and quarrels too much, and is heavily scarred from battles.

Agnes had suggested that maybe Hélène should enter an extended postulancy (pre-novitiate) so that a watch could be kept on her and her sincerity tested. If her desire was genuinely to protect her virginity and offer herself for life as a Bride of Christ, then that must be respected and of course honoured. But if she were simply avoiding an unpleasantness and opposing her parents' wishes, and intended to leave when circumstances change, that would be quite different.

It was expected that the parents would be generous with her dowry, even as they regretted her turning down their marriage arrangements. During a few weeks of postulancy, Lady Hélène proved to be genuinely devout and obedient, and showed every sign of being a credit to her community. She was accepted into the novitiate a year ago, with great satisfaction.

Sir Arsène, the rejected suitor, had been so angered by her attitude towards him that he first attempted to abduct her from the Norman abbey, and failing that, turned to assault several young peasant women on his estate, raping them and getting one of them with child. This poor girl drowned herself and her unbaptised baby in the river. Of course, churchmen consider them both to be damned for ever, but we women feel more tenderly towards them and their plight.

The Abbess was pleased to receive her and the other Sisters at Shaftesbury. However, Eulalia harboured a fear, not so much that Sister Hélène would bolt, but that Sir Arsène may try to follow her here and attempt another abduction as he had at Caen.

Eulalia: Visit of Earl-Bishop Odo, 1080

After entertaining important visitors in the years after my arrival — enjoyably in the recent case of Archbishop Lanfranc and less so in the earlier one of Queen Edith — it was another year before the next significant guest arrived.

This guest was a man who is half-brother to the King and is both the Bishop of Bayeux and the Earl of Kent. Lord Odo is also the most powerful and wealthy man in the land after the King and Queen, or was until a few years ago. As full brother to dear Sir Robert who befriended us at Corfe when we arrived, I felt we needed to welcome him with every aspect of friendship and hospitality. While I used to think him a great friend, as he had been somewhat generous to our Abbey of the Trinity as Caen, I have since revised my opinion of him as a good man. Since the Conquest he has succumbed to the temptation of cupidity, rapaciously acquiring lands and enormous wealth.

When the King is away from England, he gives his kinsman regency power, but Odo has taken advantage of that to prosper himself.

My dear friend Lanfranc, on becoming Archbishop of Canterbury, determined to retrieve some of the treasures taken from the cathedral by Odo. In 1076 he forced a three-day trial at Penenden Heath at which Odo defended himself against Bishop Geoffrey de Montbray, representing the King, and Archbishop Lanfranc himself prosecuting for the Church. There were several other bishops and nobles present, some with great knowledge of law. The outcome meant Bishop Odo returning much of the lands and possessions that he had — I hate to say it of a man of the Church — stolen.

The Earl-Bishop was passing through Shaftesbury from seeing his brother in Corfe and was going on to Malmesbury and thence to Gloucester, where he had much business to attend.

Of course I and my Obedientes welcomed him with every show of hospitality, while his large retinue was lodged with Sir Thibault and others in the town, according to their rank. We went straightaway into the chapel for Sir Bertin to intone the Te Deum in thanks for the safe arrival of the visiting party. On the way there, after visiting the latrine house, Lord Odo seemed so listless and depressed, so unlike his usual boisterous self, that I asked him what troubled him. He thought a little of what he should say, then told me that, while staying in Corfe, he had been put in oversight of evictions in what has been designated, the 'Nova Foresta' (New Forest). The King had decided that a great tract of land in Wessex between Winchester and Christchurch should be developed as a royal hunting forest and would be better for hunting game without being troubled by the Saxons living there.

"Under me, some two thousand peasants will be driven from their villages and hovels in the next few years. This requires a great deal of effort I assure you," he said with passion. "Their buildings have to be thoroughly destroyed as well as their patches of crops where they have cleared the forest."

I expressed sympathy with the arduousness of the task.

"What is more," he added, "I have to oversee the limbs or ears cut off from those Saxons who unlawfully poach deer or hares from the royal forest or try to resist their evictions — necessary, but such unpleasant work." I shuddered, then tried to raise his spirits by assuring him that staying here for a week or so would help him recover his spirits and humour. I was pleasantly surprised at the noble bishop's sensitivity, knowing how brutally he and Bishop Geoffrey de Montbray (just before the latter turned against him) treated the followers of the rebellious Ralph de Guader, Earl of East

Anglia in 1075, ordering the right foot to be cut off each defeated man.

After prayers in the chapel, Sir Bertin asked to speak with him alone, with which request we complied — though I had some anxiety about what our priest might divulge to the Earl-Bishop.

I need not have worried! While Sister Anise, our Hospitaless, was taking Odo to his guest quarters, Sir Bertin approached me, beaming happily and holding up a coin-bag like a hard-won trophy.

"Mother Eulalia", for now he and some others called me that, "See! The good Bishop has given me enough gold here that now I can employ a deacon and a subdeacon to help me during liturgy as my obligations are growing daily. Is that not good news?" I was not sure. I think I was irritated, vexed even, that he had not consulted me before asking for outside funding. I had already agreed that he needed help, as the town was recovering and pilgrims beginning to return, so he could no longer use the uneducated masspriests in the town.

Nevertheless, it is my duty to appoint my clergy and see that they were suitably funded. Had I not recently appointed four prebendary chaplains to the various local churches at Gillingham, Fontmell Magna, Iweren Minster and Liddington? I did not like the idea of Earl Odo thinking that I was not supporting the Church. I think I shall recruit another chaplain, one to myself and leave Sir Bertin to the Abbey as a whole. He might be more use in managing the estate as Steward Thibault tells me that he is not really useful. He is too self-indulgent and careless of the interests of others. Why, the proceeds of shipwrecks off the coast of Dorset belong to us, but he rarely pursues them and Steward Thibault is too busy to be concerned with everything.

I smiled weakly and nodded, leaving him not too sure of my reaction. That should keep him from further presumption.

Fortunately, the funding for Bertin did not exhaust our guest's generosity. He brought us gifts from his brother, Count Robert, and greetings from the King himself.

What he was particularly excited about were the designs and plans for his new cathedral in Bayeux — a splendid Norman-Romanesque edifice, such as the one I intend to raise here in Shaftesbury. When I mentioned the potential costs of our project, he instantly produced a purse of gold coin and handed it over with a broad smile. What a friend to our Abbey! What a good man he is. How could I have thought otherwise!

After a hearty meal taken privately with Sir Bertin, the two men joined the Obedientes and me in the chapter-house where, over wine and cider refreshment, our visitor regaled us with anecdotes and stories from his colourful and eventful life. He described how he had fought heroically in the great victory at Hastings, armed only with a mace, for clerics, as you know, are forbidden the use of spear or sword. He tells of the heads he cracked and of one Saxon whose eyes fell out, such was the force of the weight struck upon the back of his head! Oh, how he laughed. Prioress Cecilia and I caught each other's eye, but said nothing.

In a more serious tone he advised me not to be too concerned about the attitude of the Saxons here, for in time, he said, they would become like us in speech, dress and manners — just as the Britons had once adapted to Roman rule in this land, wearing the toga and learning Latin, becoming more civilised Roman than they were savage Briton. We must convince them, he told us, that our superior culture will bring them more benefits than their own.

'If they cannot be convinced by gentle means, they must be made afraid — fear often wins where arguments do not,' he said. He may be right — he is a great man and a bishop after all.

Since being here I had learned of the way the Saxons had organised themselves as a society and conducted justice, which seemed actually superior to our Norman customs. I understand that King William is likewise impressed and intends to keep much of the social organisation as it had been. I doubt Bishop Odo, clever though he is, quite appreciates this.

The next day, our esteemed guest sent for something magnificent he had left in the care of his two most trusted servants.

We cleared the long tables in the refectory and laid two of them end to end to roll out on them the wonderful fabric he showed us with great pride. It was a very long cloth, 75 yards or so, but not very high, less than two feet. It was far too long for all of it to be seen at once, so at one end two Sisters unrolled it and at the other end two Sisters carefully rolled it up, while we (the rest of the Norman nuns and some of the Saxons) all crowded round it to view the incidents described in coloured thread. It took us no little time to view it entirely, and some Sisters, very excited, wanted to see it all again in order to take it all in. It felt as though we were in the middle of the events themselves!

Even the narrow top and bottom border depicted delightful and fantastic birds and beasts, plus stories from Aesop's Fables and hunting scenes as well as illustrations of various farming practices. Really these Saxon nuns and monks can certainly sew! The names of the Saxons given on the work are spelled in the way of their tongue, with 'th's looking like leaning over crossed 'd's.

The main theme was to show our King's great victory over the Saxons at Hastings, and even the Bishop is depicted, wielding his mace. It had been commissioned by the nobleman Eustace of Boulogne, in Kent, and presented to Odo to display when his new abbey in Bayeux opens. This Eustace is also shown in the battle pointing to Duke William as the latter raises his helmet to prove he was indeed alive.

The Bishop is greatly pleased with it and is proud to own such a record. He is taking it around to those monasteries and abbeys in which, like ours, he takes an interest, to show to the communities. I admit to being a little troubled by parts of it but did not speak of my misgivings to the Bishop for fear of quenching his happiness.

What I noticed was that the Saxon warlord Harold Godwinson was called 'Rex', and there was an illustration of his coronation by an archbishop. Surely that supports the claim, which we consider false, of his being the rightful monarch after Edward the Confessor, and undermines the claim of our own Duke William? We all know that Harold had sworn allegiance to William, admittedly under duress as a hostage at Mont-Saint-Michel, but nevertheless swearing over holy relics made it a sacred oath. When he returned to England, the ignorant Saxon council, known here as the Witmangemot, elected him king. No wonder King Edward the Confessor's chosen successor and cousin, our William, was obliged to seek his rightful inheritance by force.

In another place, Norman knights are shown pillaging the land as soon as they arrive on shore, whereas Harold is shown, when he was a hostage of William, heroically rescuing Normans from drowning in quicksand. These elements seem to me to verge on the subversive — but somehow Bishop Odo does not see them.

On the last evening of the visit, and as it was full summer-time, we placed trestle tables outside, within the enclosure but not the cloistered quarters. This was so that we could invite the bishop's senior retainers and their hosts to a celebratory feast. My Obedientes and I, with Sir Bertin, welcomed the guests and I knew, though could not see, that many of our Sisters would be peering through the cloister windows and fencing to catch an excited glimpse of the glamorous and gallant company. Some of the local hosts were accompanied by their wives and older sons or daughters. The bishop himself looked resplendent in cloth of gold and intricately embroidered robes, and all were dressed in their most sumptuous garments. Sir Thibault had hired a couple of musicians, a lutenist who also sang, and a shawm player, to entertain us. It really was a magnificent occasion, with food and drink to match — thanks largely to the benevolence of our guest who insisted on providing the superb wine. Noblemen and servants swarmed the ground where usually the geese and hens grazed, and all was colour, light and laughter.

My attention was taken during the feast in entertaining our principal guests, so when Prioress Cecilia called me aside to voice an anxiety over something, I was at first annoyed to be so distracted. However, what she told me was highly concerning.

"Mother, I have noticed two of the Bishop's men, in their red cloaks, going behind the church, looking furtively around."

"Gracious, what would they be doing there? They cannot need to relieve themselves as the latrine house is just over there."

"I think they may be making for the cloister — that's my fear."

I instantly asked the Bishop for the names of those of his retainers wearing red cloaks.

"Why," he replied, "they are dear friends of mine — all good fighters and high born. There is Sir Ralph d'Aufrey and Sir Arsène of Sourdeval, and ....."

I heard no more than that for panic had arisen into my gorge, and I let out a little cry and "No, no!"

Bishop Odo was just sounding forth about the general sinfulness of women and how even strong and holy men sometimes cannot withstand the temptations they pose. He did not notice my standing and rushing over to rouse Sir Thibault and Sheriff Fitzgrip until those two knights leapt up from their benches and buckled on their swords. The other guests watched silently as the two went off chasing after the miscreants. After a few minutes they returned, bringing one red-faced and red-cloaked knight at sword point between them. Sheriff Fitzgrip carried another red cloak folded over his arm.

"Sir Ralph! What were you doing back there?" demanded his lord, Earl-Bishop Odo.

"Ralph?" I asked, with rising panic, "Then where is Arsène, Sir Arsène of Sourdeval?"

Sir Ralph D'Aufrey then chilled my heart by denying he knew where. The two men had indeed intended to breach the cloister and abduct the Lady Hélène but in the scuffle just now, he had not seen what had become of his friend.

The Prioress and I soon found the lady with all the other novices safe within their dormitory, but of the Norman knight there was no sign. He must have fled.

There was but one thing to do, and that before the Bishop left the next day, and that was to see the Lady Hélène fully professed as a Sister which would prevent any future abduction. It could not guarantee it, as there were regrettably several instances of even royal men taking nuns by force from their convents. But it should discourage Sir Arsène of Sourdeval, we hoped.

The following morning, therefore, after Mass in the chapel, we processed to the chapter house where Bishop Odo, in full and sumptuous vestments, sat on the abbatial throne, with me on his right and Prioress Cecilia on his left, and heard the three vows of the young woman. The first, Stabilitas, *bound her to this particular community for life; the second was the* Conversatio morum, *whereby she vowed to live a life fitting for a nun, which includes lifelong singleness, chastity and a frugal lifestyle; the third,* Obedentia *—and I deliberately caught her eye while she swore this — is wherein her duty of obedience to the Rule of St Benedict and to her religious superiors is modelled on that of Christ to His Father. In the next rite, being a consecrated virgin, she has a* mitra *or crown placed on her head and a ring on her marriage finger. These symbolic actions indicate her becoming a Sposa Christi or Bride of Christ as is the Church as a whole (Ephesians 5:22-33).*

When all was done, the bishop retired to the sacristy to disrobe and assume once more the costume of a traveller, albeit one of great wealth and high rank.

A Dangerous Journey

Shortly after the departure of Bishop Odo I had to make a journey myself. There were two reasons for it. One was that a new Abbess was being installed in Wilton Abbey and I was invited. Shaftesbury was the nearest women's abbey in distance as well as in wealth and influence, being awarded the status of barony, a rare honour granted to very few women's abbeys. I would have sent my Prioress to represent me had there not been another reason for me to go in person, although Wilton is so Saxon that I find it quite disagreeable.

The young Flemish monk Goscelin, a close friend of Bishop Herman, was residing at Wilton, and had written a Life of their most illustrious Saint Edith (not, I hasten to add, the widow of Edward the Confessor, who visited us the year before she died). I had met this monk at my installation and, excited by how his Lives of saints makes pilgrimages to their relic-shrines highly popular, I had commissioned him to write about our own Saint Edward. He had travelled about the county investigating accounts of the wonders and healings performed by our saint, and had visited Shaftesbury a few times, talking with the pilgrims and the priests who said Masses for them. I was impatient to read the results of his researches in his Passion of St Edward, King and Martyr and of how he exalts the virtues of the saint and the power of his intercession.

I set off on horseback with a select party of nuns, both

Norman and Saxon, and accompanied by Sheriff Fitzgrip and six of his armed men to cross Cranborne Chase following a route through forest and pastureland. Fortunately this journey does not involve lots of steep hillsides but is remote from settlements and villages of any note. Having travelled from early morning, by the time the sun was high we planned to stop at the next clearing to stretch our legs, eat our vittles, and give the horses a short break.

However, the horses knew something was wrong before we did. Their neighing and skittering alerted us to trouble, so that straightaway four of the Sheriff's warriors placed themselves in the vanguard while two protected the back of our line. Shortly afterwards, as we entered a clearing, a row of hostile savages, some mounted, others on foot, confronted us, weapons pointing at us. They began their approach, shouting to each other and brandishing their spears, battleaxes and seaxes most threateningly. I crossed myself and prayed aloud, calling on all the saints to intercede for us and save us. As I did so, and saw my fellow Norman Sisters ashen with fear, one of the Saxon nuns, our novice mistress, Sister Tibba, urged her horse forward, despite the soldiers' alarmed protests, and rode up to the leader of these shaggy barbarians. As she spoke with him, his men lowered their weapons and relaxed their stance.

Sheriff Fitzgrip whispered to the nearest soldier, and I heard him say "Now let's at them. Take them off guard."

I called out "No! No, wait!" and prevented unnecessary

bloodshed, as Sister Tibba waved to us to dismount and approach in peace. She came to me and bade the leader come to be introduced. While both sides dismounted and made wary but non-aggressive contact with each other, she presented the man to me.

"Mother Eulalia," she said smiling, "this is Lord Alwyn. He and I are related although we have not met for a long while. He is a Saxon thegn and until recently fought alongside Hereward the Wake." I recoiled at the sound of that frightful name — the rebel leader who had terrorised the Norman communities and monks in the east of England. However, I thought it politic to control my apprehension and let her continue.

"No, Madame, really, he is no monster I assure you. He is a Christian and supports the poor and weak."

I snorted at that. "Indeed," I replied, "so why be prepared to attack our small convoy of nuns?"

The two then spoke awhile together in their tongue. Then Sister Tibba, more downcast and hesitant than a few moments earlier, explained.

"Alwyn and his men were taking shelter in these woods, deciding whether to join Hereward in his exile, going North, or take the southern route and escape over to Flanders, when they were set upon by a wandering Norman knight and a halfdozen of his followers. They fought hard and both sides shed blood and lost men. Seeing Sheriff Fitzgrip's soldiers, they thought they were more of this band returning to avenge their dead leader."

"Is there a name of this leader, this knight?" I had a moment's hope, and then it was confirmed. From the mouth of Alwyn came the name of the slain knight over whom I would shed no tears. "Sir Arsène of Sourdeval," he announced.

Soon we were all sitting around, women on logs, men on the ground, handing round skins of beer and pieces of bread and cheese which we had brought for the journey. We made a promise of mutual respect. We would say nothing of this encounter, nor of the story we had heard, and in exchange, these Saxons would give us safe passage as far as Barford St Martin and then leave us to cover the last few miles without them. They would also ensure that all Saxons roundabout would enable us to pass safely in future. As there could well be other hostile gangs and outlaws lurking in the forests, we were grateful for their protection.

I held Sister Tibba in rather higher regard than previously, and she began to become more of a confidante than any other Saxon. I consulted her almost daily and was gratified to learn that the Saxon Sisters were becoming accustomed to our Norman ways and more acceptable of changes. I was able to increase the severity of penances imposed on them for their daily sins and imperfections, and Sister Tibba reported that they were not resentful. The novices, both of Norman and Saxon stock, were well instructed and all but a very few went on to full profession.

Chronicle: Another Royal Visitor: Queen Matilda, 1081

In 1078 Bishop Herman died and the Abbess took the opportunity to invite his chaplain, Sir Robert, to become her own. Sir Bertin was not best pleased, and tried to ingratiate himself with the new Bishop, Osmund, now based at Sarum instead of Sherborne. If he had hoped to become a canon, he was disappointed. This new bishop was a friend of Archbishop Lanfranc and intended only the most learned and disciplined of canons to form a new cathedral chapter. He was right to ignore Bertin, as the future reputation of Sarum as a centre of scholarship would not have been enhanced by his presence!

Queen Matilda had been writing letters to Abbess Eulalia since her appointment, one that was largely engineered by the Queen. But latterly the letters were more frantic and desperate, begging Eulalia for her prayers and those of the whole community. For years the poor Queen had suffered by the behaviour of her sons.

She had lost her highly-loved second son Richard as a sixteen-year-old in 1070 in a riding accident, but two of the others, Robert Curthose ("short boots" a term of endearment coined in his infancy by his father) and William Rufus (having red or ginger hair), were constantly quarrelling — both between themselves and with their father.

The two younger boys, William and Henry, once upturned a full chamber pot over the head of Robert, who was furious with them and maddened that his father did not punish them. Whoever heard of royal princes behaving in such a way!

Robert then even instigated an armed rebellion against his father, attempting to capture the city of Rouen. His father tried to arrest him, but he fled to his uncle in Flanders, causing trouble wherever he went. His poor mother had to send him money and support secretly, but when William found this out, there was a mighty row!

Anyway, the Queen informed the Abbess of her intended visit — a rare blessing, as she rarely left Normandy. The King and Queen were travelling from Winchester up to Gloucester with Archbishop Lanfranc, and Matilda left them after Salisbury to join us for a night. She would meet up with them at Malmesbury.

One day at noon in December, when the wintry sun was attempting to pierce a heavy mass of dark grey clouds, the Queen's party arrived with relatively little show. The Queen and a few of her ladies were escorted by a dozen armed soldiers, led by Sheriff Fitzgrip and Count Robert of Mortain and latterly of Corfe. The men removed themselves on handing over the royal ladies to the care of the Abbey community, until they were needed the following day.

The Queen greeted Abbess Eulalia warmly and explained that her visit to Malmesbury was at the behest of Osmond, the new Bishop of Salisbury. He was keen to promote the cult of Saint Aldhelm at Malmesbury, where the relics of the saint were preserved. The Queen was supporting that devotion to a newly canonised Saxon saint by handing over her lands at Garsdon to that abbey — rather to our Abbess's chagrin.

"Now then," chided her royal guest, with a smile, "I hope that look does not signify envy that I am endowing that abbey and not your own?"

Before Eulalia could rebuff the suggestion, although it stung in its accuracy, the Queen continued,

"After all, yours has more wealth than the abbeys of Cerne and Malmesbury combined! Or even than Romsey, Nunnaminster and Amesbury combined! You know you can always count on our support if times are ever hard. And I send you the daughters of our richest nobles with their generous dowries, do I not?"

The Abbess coloured and admitted all of that was true and that she was very grateful.

There passed between them long conversations and times of prayer together which the Abbess has instructed me not to record, being confidential and concerning both the troubled family of the monarch and the problems the King and Lanfranc were having with the Pope in Rome. It seems Pope Gregory was demanding that all worldly kings should pay homage to him and not choose the bishops and abbots in their countries. The German Emperor was so enraged that he had just elected his own Pope — so now there were two! What was a good Catholic to do? The Queen's visit certainly caused the Abbess many sleepless nights following this news.

There are only two anecdotes I can relate, as I was there when they were told and no one told me not to record them. One concerns the late widow of Edward the Confessor, Queen Edith. She had a hatred of Matilda, calling her, in a charter in 1072, William's mistress! ("Mathyld, his gebedde"), so in the charter Matilda is presenting in Malmesbury she makes a point of calling herself "Queen and legal wife of William"! She laughed merrily at Eulalia's account of the haughty Saxon queen's visit to the abbey some years before.

She also told the story of Edith's favourite courtier, the wealthy and handsome Brihtric Mau. King Edward sent him to Flanders when Matilde was still in her father's court there, aged about sixteen. She fell in love with the young nobleman and as he left, and defying parents, reputation and sense, she sent him a proposal of marriage. He rejected it, the brute! Anyway, now, years later, she is Queen and demanded the manor of

Tewkesbury from Brihtric, deprived his town of Gloucester of its charter and even had him imprisoned. How she and Eulalia laughed! She said how she would like to have been there at the moment of his arrest — just as a chapel he had built was about to be consecrated, with the Bishop of Worcester all ready to perform the ceremony.

Queen Matilda's visit was all too short and was almost the last of great note in the lifetime of the Abbess. Several mighty matters of state took place between the Queen's visit and the death of the Abbess — especially the turbulence following the death of the King in 1087 when his sons fought each other over the succession, Robert being passed over for the throne of England on account of his former bad behaviour, and William Rufus reigning for a few years until, like his oldest brother, he was accidentally killed in a riding accident, also in the New Forest. He was succeeded by the youngest brother, Henry. However, these matters scarcely impinged upon the life of the Abbey as the community concentrated on their spiritual and charitable duties.

However, one national event occurred that did concern the Abbey after the death of Queen Matilda in 1083 and before that of her husband in 1087. The King had ordered a great survey of all the land.

Eulalia: The Great Survey of 1086

Sir Thibault, my High Steward, has been summoned by King's commissioners to convene a court of local landowners. He has had to clear the courtroom next to the gatehouse, where tenants pay their fees in coin or kind, and where penalties are extracted for infringements of laws. Normally local trials for the Sixpenny (Seaxpenn, "hill of the Saxons") Handley (hēan "high"; lēage "clearing") Hundred, are held there. They usually involve few persons, but now a considerable number have been called upon — no burgesses, but leading freemen, especially those holding manors. Apparently every shire in the land is being surveyed by agents under Ranulf Flambard, a favourite courtier and the son of a priest of Bayeux. The King has instructed him to catalogue who exactly has his holdings, owes him dues and, in particular, can produce for him knights and fighting men at a time of war.

Sir Thibault is a careful, thorough man and firmly believes that the King is right to order this survey, although there are many who object. I feel that the Saxons feel it a violation of their ancient rights — although all the land in the country now belongs to the King — while the Normans fear they and their sons will not escape military duties if the King knows all. I admit to feeling there is something unnatural about noting every detail of every landholding — a certain betrayal of the relationship between people and land. Of course, we hold a similar record of all that the Abbey possesses. Nevertheless, there seems a difference between men with soil on their hands and men with quills in theirs, that cannot be easily reconciled.

I met one of the Commissioners' clerks, a young Piers de Pevensey, born in England shortly after the Conquest, and invited him to talk as we walked around the enclosure. He told me the book he was helping to compile, the Liber de Wintonia *(Book of Winchester, later known as the* Domesday Book) *would be kept in the royal treasury and referred to as needed. I asked what it was he needed to know, and he told me that he and his colleagues were holding sworn inquests everywhere, asking questions in three categories. These concerned how land had been held: as it had been on the last day of the reign of Edward the Confessor (5 January 1066); as it had been when it was granted by King William; and finally as it is now when the survey is taken.*

I asked what sort of questions, to which he replied, "Such as who held it and now holds it? How many hides does it comprise? How much land and how many oxen has each tenant-in-chief, freeman, sokeman, and how many villeins, slaves and cottagers there are on each holding? That sort of thing."

I expressed surprise at the amount of detail required and he agreed that it was tiring work and that his writing hand ached from so much scribbling. "Especially here", he added, "as the Abbey itself holds so many manors in Dorset and beyond".

When he left to continue his work, I sent for Prioress Cecilia to ask for her opinion on all this information gathering. Margot, for it was she I sent, returned wailing — so I knew the news was bad.

"Oh Abbess, my Lady! Sister Cecilia is not at all well. She cannot speak, her face is all pulled down on one side. Nor can she move, although one hand and arm waves about. She looks about her but sees nothing! Oh my Lady — has the Devil taken her?"

This began the saddest time, when my companion of old, my nearest and dearest friend in the community, was disabled of the power of speech. She made some recovery, so that in time she could limp about and feed herself with one good arm, but her senses were gone and a few sounds she uttered were more like grunts and groans than words. She was still the same gentle person she had been, but I mourned the loss of her shining intelligence.

I replaced her as Prioress by Sister Agnes, who had come over with Lady Helene and had the experience of responsibility at Caen. She did not last long in that position, as I found she was lazy and neglectful of her duties. She would be found asleep during meditation and allowed the Sisters to talk at times of silence. I reprimanded her and demoted her to the charge of the children, the oblates and others who had been sent here for education. There would be little opportunity for her to doze off with a dozen pairs of young eyes upon her. Her Latin and grammar were sufficient to the task, and indeed she rather flourished in the role.

The position of Prioress I gave to a Norman, Cecily, daughter of Baron Robert of Fitzhamon. Not only did her name remind me of dear Cecilia, but she was like her in many ways too — intelligent, shrewd, good-humoured and devout. I suspect she will make a good Abbess after I am gone.

Sister Astrid, the half-Dane, half-Saxon Sister whose admiration of King Cnut had drawn her here, soon took a great interest too in St Edward and the history of the Abbey, from the time of its foundation by King Aldred's daughter Aethelgifu. I permitted Astrid to correspond with the neighbouring Religious Houses for information, although any records held in the women's Abbey at Wimborne had been lost when it succumbed to Viking onslaught in 1013. The secular canons who live there now have been as helpful as they could be. Astrid is now the female pilgrims' guide, relating stories about St Edward and encouraging devotion to his cult. I am pleased to have been right in accepting her into our community and she is obedient to my command that she does not fraternise with male pilgrims, but that if they come in a party with women, she can include them in her instruction.

PART FOUR
THE STORY CONCLUDES, 1086-1107

Chronicle: Abbey Life

A well-run abbey is not eventful. It follows a regular pattern during each day and night, with feast days and fast days and the natural seasons causing only expected minor changes of clothing, timings and apparel.

This Abbey was well run, with Mother Eulalia establishing it as a place of quiet industry and learning. The Saxon Sisters now all spoke Norman French fluently, and the newcomers from either background are made to feel welcome by all. The separate dining and sleeping arrangements were abandoned, and everyone lived together in harmony — most of the time. Small disagreements inevitably cropped up, but none lasted long. Very few Sisters left the community, and usually only because of the pressing demands of ageing family members.

The trees and vines the early Norman community had planted on their arrival were now mature and fruitful; the hospital had gained a reputation for the Sisters' knowledge of the healing power of herbs, and the pilgrim shrines for the healing power of the divine intercession of its saints. Many of the children who had been educated here returned to visit, now clerics or nuns. Some were neither but appreciated the learning and skills they had acquired here. Indeed, the Abbey flourished both spiritually and materially through the good and wise guidance of its Abbess. She, like the other surviving Sisters of that tumultuous crossing in 1074, was less vigorous and more inclined to suffer ill-health. She seemed to become calmer in spirit, but rather more melancholy as she grew older.

Eulalia: The Visit and Friendship of Archbishop Anselm, 1094

The only consolation towards the end of my life was the friendship of the monk Anselm, Abbot of Bec, whom I had known briefly during my Novitiate. Grown important, through his wisdom, scholarship and Christian leadership, he was now Archbishop of Canterbury since the death in 1089 of my dear friend Lanfranc. Anselm was always his protégé and it was right for him to follow him into the highest clerical position in the land, even though there was a four year gap — William Rufus being notorious in his reluctance to make new church appointments whenever they became vacant, as he could meanwhile take all their revenues for himself. I speak critically of royalty like that, because Anselm himself, like Lanfranc his mentor, was not afraid of challenging secular authority where he saw it was necessary.

He visited the Abbey but once. That was last year, but he kindly kept in touch with me by letter and told me that he had heard many good reports of me and my reforms here in Shaftesbury from Archbishop Lanfranc, and to my surprise and delight, from Queen Matilda.. They both spoke warmly of the steps we had taken since our earliest days here to make this Abbey one of the greatest in the land in faith as well as in wealth.

When I saw him approach, I was quite surprised to see his once-black curly hair, that surrounded his tonsure like a nest around an egg, now white, but still thickly curled. His face, red from the exhaustion of walking, leading his horse, shone with warmth and friendliness. He seemed to find meeting me again, after so long, a very great joy. I was thrilled! He handed over his panting and sweating horse to one of the gatekeepers and embraced me with a hug. So very Italian!

I asked about the Earl-Bishop Odo who had once visited here and of whom I had not heard for a while. Anselm told me how, in 1082 King William was obliged to imprison his half brother. It seems the Bishop was planning an armed raid on Rome to make himself Pope, and had to be put away for everyone's sake. He stayed in prison for five years, since when he caused trouble for William's successor and was banished to Normandy. He has not been actively heard of, but is rumoured to be planning to go on crusade to the Holy Land.

I could see that the Archbishop preferred not of talk of such worldly matters, despite being so involved in the governance of the country. His heart is in theology, as is mine.

During his visit we spoke at length on such topics as which comes first, faith or understanding and he argued well for faith being the basis on which to build understanding, whereas I had suggested that you needed to understand something in order to believe in it. I also brought up with him the dilemma one of our novices had expressed and which I could not answer. "If God knows all," she had asked, "then what need has He of our prayers? We tell Him how we revere Him, and hope for this or that at His gracious hand, and so on. But surely He knows all that already?"

Dear Anselm suggested that I should answer: "While God has no need of our prayers, for indeed He knows all that we say and think, yet we have need of praying to Him!"

Without prayer, I took that to mean, we would behave like God and think ourselves on His level, and yet, as Anselm also explained, God is greater than anything we can imagine. We cannot conceive of anything greater — in perfections, in virtues, in goodness, in creativity, than Him whom we call God.

This God has provided sinful mankind with an example of human sinlessless in the Virgin Mary, Mother of God's own Son, Jesus. I nodded, not quite understanding what he was implying. By the gift of this woman, uniquely without sin from her conception, we nuns, so he taught me, have a perfect model to which to aspire. It is our mission to imitate, as closely as is possible for us, her holiness and her obedience. We must cultivate harmony within our lives together. He gave me a prayer to say that he composed, in honour of the Virgin's nativity: "Vouchsafe that I may praise thee, O sacred Virgin; give me strength against thine enemies, and against the enemy of the whole human race."

I came away from converse with him with so much to think about and with a conviction to pray better and with more sincerity. It put me in mind of a strange other-worldly experience I had earlier in my time here but am not sure that it should be recorded. I ordered books of his theology for our library in the hope that our younger Sisters might learn something of his insights and scholarship.

I received several letters from Anselm over the years, and one in particular struck me as gracious and loving.

It arrived a few months after his visit. In it he expressed his love for us all in Shaftesbury and equates my authority here with his own, although he has so much more responsibility. I was much touched by that, and by his humble request for our prayers. His teaching us concerns our striving for the upward path to heaven, which he acknowledges that we have already begun. He is such a generous and thoughtful man, and with so many worldly concerns yet he finds the time to write such encouragement to us!

Chronicle: A Private Note (Vision)

The following is something which the Abbess recalls as happening early on in her Abbacy and has allowed me to record, but then states that she does not wish it to become public. In one way it shines a glorious light on our dear Abbess, but in another, it contains a reprimand which is uncomfortable, to say the least. This is it, but if you prefer, skip over it until the next passage of Chronicle.

Eulalia

Sister, you can write down my words, but I am not decided whether you should include them in your chronicle.

You know how impatient I was at the beginning with the Saxon Sisters stumbling over the Latin prayers and dragging out the responses — through their typical linguistic reluctance or ignorance, or both. I was obliged to send for that Brother Roland from Cluny Abbey to teach them the proper Gregorian Chant and Sir Bertin to teach them Latin. I admit to chivvying them up by leading the prayers quite quickly. I would pray, and then see who was still struggling with the words. I would speak with them afterwards and direct them to spend more time and effort on their Latin lessons.

Anyhow, I had been taking myself most nights to the little church, the one we used before moving into our great one. It was quiet then, without the constant sound of masonry hammers and workmen's shouts. I would pray for two or three hours or so, in the kneeling position with my hands clasped, not open and raised in the old style.

For many nights I had the feeling that I was not alone in there, and yet when I looked around I could see even in the deep gloom, that there was no other person, Saxon or Norman, religious or lay. Yet I sensed the presence of a woman. Why a woman? I cannot tell.

Well, one night, after fasting for two days and really

concentrating on my prayers, that sense I had actually materialised in a dazzling light — and in a woman's form. Yet what a woman did I see! With my own eyes I looked upon the face and form of our heavenly Mother, Theotakos, the Holy Mother of God! St Mary herself. This vision, this apparition looked at me, right into my eyes. Then, this is what is almost incredible, she spoke! My heart was so thudding and pulsating in my ears that I could hardly hear what she said.

She spoke my name, "Eulalia, Eulalia, my child". Her Norman French was perfect.

I held my breath wondering what glimpse of our eternal home, what aspect of divine majesty at the court of the Heavenly King she would describe. What great truth would she reveal or promise of future reward or punishment?

Imagine my surprise, however, when she uttered her next words,

"Eulalia," she said in the gentlest of tones, "my dear, do not gabble the words of prayers addressed to me. Do not rush through the Ave Maria, *the prayer which honours both me and my beloved Son."*

With that, the vision vanished, and I found myself laughing out loud. I laughed long and loud — such was my relief and yet my surprise.

Then I wept, great tears rolled down my cheeks and dampened the head cloth around my neck. For my prayers, my humble little prayers, both those said in community and alone, were indeed heard in heaven. I had assurance of that.

Not only were they heard, but they caused pain, for it seemed that they were not properly respectful.

I felt remorse — terrible remorse for causing discomfort to our Mother in heaven. More than any Queen on earth, she is the One who should be truly honoured.

I made a solemn vow that very night, that not only would I pray more slowly, with more reverence, but I would myself teach, patiently and gently, all the Saxon nuns here to pronounce their words more correctly and easily. That will be my penance.

Chronicle: Changes of Personnel, 1104

The Abbey is a sad place. Several of the nuns who came over with Eulalia have died, and the Abbess herself is in poor health. Her constant coughing keeps her awake, and she has to absent herself at times from the Office. Even at Mass, she occasionally has to leave the church to cough outside so as not to disturb the others. Sister Tibba has taken over more and more responsibilty as she is sub-Prioress to Prioress Agnes, who lacks the energy of Tibba. In fact she has little energy at all and is known to fall asleep during times of meditation.

There is a new Steward, Sir Victor, appointed after the death of Sir Thibault, and he is thorough, or rather ruthless, in his pursuit of collecting rents and dues. An unpleasant, unsmiling man, he ordered the blinding of two of the poachers on Abbey lands, until the Abbess got to hear of it and stopped the practice. Aubrey, our Cellaress, has asked to be transferred to another post as she finds working with Sir Victor depresses her spirits. A recently professed Saxon, Sister Aluvena is being considered to take her place. This young woman displays no end of good cheer, if being a little giddy and prone to giggling, but has a solid grasp of the duties required. How the two will work together with sub-Prioress Tibba will be interesting to behold.

Sir Bertin is not much missed and the new Abbey Chaplain, Sir Arturo, in charge of a deacon and two sub-deacons, is a great improvement. The liturgies are so much better conducted and more in accordance with the best Benedictine abbeys. Sir Robert, the Abbess's personal Chaplain, a good and clever man, has time to spare in the scriptorium, where his skills and knowledge are much appreciated.

Abbess Eulalia now has two personal servants but deeply misses the late Margot as well as all her other old companions. The only friend she feels able to rely upon is Archbishop Anselm, whose dialogues in Rome with the Greek Catholic Church she learnt about with interest. He had left England for three years, no longer able to take the problems between King William Rufus and the Pope in Rome. Both want to be in charge of clergy appointments in England and in control of the Church here. Anselm had wanted to resign his archbishopric but Pope Urban refused to accept that. The King however confiscated all his revenues and threatened to fine him heavily. Yet Anselm refused to allow the Pope to excommunicate the King, such is his generous nature.

He returned in 1100 after his first period away but was feeling tremendous pressure again under the new King, Henry, and has again taken himself off to Lyons. The Church Council he called in London two years ago achieved great success in reforming the liturgy throughout the land, making it comply with the Gregorian rite in Rome. Through this Council Anselm also banned clergy from having wives and mistresses and becoming drunk. He also banned the practice of clergy holding more than one church appointment at the same time, and — importantly for us, banned the institution of slavery, a Saxon practice we found most distasteful. We had little to do with slaves in Shaftesbury, and in 1086 there was a group of eighteen in our grange at Bradford on Avon to whom we gave manumission. The cousin of the Abbess, Thomas, who was her main tenant at Bradford, made sure that this was done.

While he is away Archbishop Anselm has sent another letter, and the Abbess and I discussed it together at length but with no-one else. While we had asked about his proposed return there seems a certain nervousness in his replies, for he does not answer us directly, and hints that he has concerns over the safety of written correspondence. We detected the sense of threat and danger he must be experiencing, and the exhortation to rely on the protection of our guardian angels, in what he suggests are dangerous times, increases our concern for him. We know that Pope Paschal has excommunicated all bishops appointed by the King and that in revenge, the King has forbidden Anselm to return to England. After Anselm's support of King Henry when his brother Robert Curthose attempted an invasion, the ingratitude of His Majesty is shocking.

We sense that Anselm is perhaps a little envious of our position as women, "daughters" living quiet, private lives and being subject to our loving "mother", while he, as a man and foremost church leader, has to act as "father" on a far more public stage.

Eulalia: The Mystery Explained, December 1106

I am now far from well: Sister Edina, our Infirmaress considers that I have but weeks to live, and my chaplain Sir Robert tends to my spiritual needs assiduously. I am shriven and carried to the church for Mass every day. I am so light, they tell me, from the wasting disease from which I suffer. Still, my constant pain helps me to unite more closely with my Saviour, whose agony was borne for me and for all.

The new abbey church itself stands proud upon this hilltop. They tell me it can be seen for miles around in all directions. The chancel and transepts are complete and we await my dear friend Archbishop Anselm to come to dedicate and consecrate it. The rest of the church will, of course, take many years to complete, for even the great Abbey of the Trinity at Caen, my alma mater, is still some decades from completion. The church here will be dedicated both to St Mary, Virgin Mother of God, and is, as Anselm rightly argues, the purest and holiest of creatures, and to St Edward, King and Martyr, whose shrine we are priveged to keep. I have just received a letter from Anselm and hoped that in it he would give a date for this ceremony soon, before I die. Alas, it does not, but it does tell me that he has returned from his second exile, is safe and asks for our prayers that his return should be fruitful. The letter insists on the virtue of obedience — indeed so much so that I suspect there is something more behind it than just addressing my "daughters". I have heard of dreadful events in the world — King Henry capturing and burning the city of Bayeux; Robert of Normandy, known as Curthose, invading England and pitching a battle against his brother; the brother, Henry, defeating and imprisoning him. How their poor mother would have suffered to have known such things her children would do against each other, and so much against the Church, too. I suspect that the Archbishop is somehow referring to these. He is a peacemaker and so often torn between two great authorities, papal and royal, that obedience to the will of God and to one's divinely appointed Superior must be the ultimate rule that he is implying. God's rule before that of kings.

I am fading, and there are matters that I would dearly like to see resolved before I die. One I have mentioned is the consecration by Anselm of this great church at Shaftesbury and of all the new stone buildings that make up our abbey complex.

The other is to know, after all these years, who it was from among the Saxon Sisters so wished us harm that they poisoned the Norman community and caused the death of poor good Sister Anne-Marie. I cannot now punish the culprit but wish she would have owned up to her crime these thirty and more years ago.

I summon to my bedside all those surviving Saxon Sisters who were present at my arrival in 1074. There were five of them, and I addressed Sister Tibba as their most senior spokeswoman.

"Well, Sisters, will you now produce from among you the one who was behind this most grievous and sinful act? It is not too late, if it was one of you, to confess and receive my absolution."

Then Sister Tibba spoke, bashfully at first, but then more confidently:

"Dear Mother, we are all heartily sickened and

disgusted at what happened on that first night of the arrival of our Norman Sisters. After the expulsion of Abbess Leveva and her Obediantes, and then the destruction of nearly half the town, we could not believe that the Norman Sisters could have been sent by anyone other than the Devil. We were worked up into such hatred that not one of us, but all of us took part in that poisonous action. It was Prioress Eadifu's idea, but we all agreed and a dish was prepared with sliced dandelion root and white broom leaves and seeds, the sort that grow here abundantly. We each took some, just a pinch, and dropped it into the stewpot, with other strong herbs to mask the taste. We thought the Sisters would have trouble with their bowels and stomachs but honestly did not think anyone would die." She dropped her head and voice at this point. "It was thoughtless and wicked of us."

"It was indeed," I exclaimed in the strongest voice I could muster. There was a pause while I thought what to say next. Then I spoke again,

"How is it, after all the chapter meetings, daily over all these years, that none of you confessed this, nor sought me out for individual confession? Some of you must have gone to their death with this unshriven sin upon their souls!"

"No, Mother, for..." she looked at the others for encouragement to go on, "for, we each of us went to Sir Bertin and made the confession to him. And received his absolution."

My heart nearly expired at that moment, it beat so hard

and fast at the news of this treachery. Ordained men, monks and priests, were hearing confessions privately more and more, and the rights of women in monastic authority are being eroded. Where will it all end?

"But," I choked, "I never saw public penances for this wicked sin! No prolonged period of fasting, no prostrations, no seeking forgiveness from me and the Norman Sisters!"

"No, Mother. Sir Bertin gave us prayers to say, silently and privately, for penance and bid us not to say anything to you or any of the Sisters. He said the punishment for harming Normans by Saxons would have been terrible and cause unrest in the town and beyond. So we swore we would never admit anything to anyone....until now, dearest Mother."

Chronicle: January 1107

Abbess Eulalia died shortly after the account given above, having made her peace with all the remaining Saxon Sisters. She gave her blessing to them, even as she lay dying.

We have applied to the King to appoint Prioress Cecily as our next Abbess and while she will be a suitable leader, there is none that can compare with the gift to us all, and to Shaftesbury, of our dear Mother Eulalia.

THE DAILY PRAYER LIFE OF THE NUNS

The Hours of the Divine Office

The Office, or 'duty' (*officium*) is a set of daily services said privately or, in a religious community, said and sung/chanted collectively. The prayers are intended for their spiritual improvement but also for the sake of the world, calling for God's protection of and support for all people, living and dead. It consists of eight 'Hours', six during daytime and two together (*Matins* and *Lauds*) at night. Most medieval people slept in two stages, roughly from dusk to midnight and then, after an hour or so awake performing chores, until dawn.

The Hours are spaced out from early morning, beginning with *Prime* at dawn, after which the nuns would read in the cloister, then wash and dress into day habits and shoes. This would be followed by a meeting in the chapter-house. Then *Terce* comes at about nine after which they celebrate High Mass (for which the ordained priest-chaplain was necessary) and then work at their tasks, and *Sext* at noon before the meal of the day. After more work or study they would have *None* (pronounced as in 'known') at three pm, at six pm *Vespers* and at nine pm *Compline*. Between the last two there would be a light supper, a *collatio* taken in the chapter-house.

Around midnight the community would rise in night habits and shoes for Matins and, after silent prayer, Lauds, before returning to bed.

The routine changed slightly between summer and winter, with each Hour comprising psalms and hymns, prayers and readings from Scripture and the early Church Fathers. The whole Psalter of 150 psalms would be recited over the course of a week, with some repeated during the week. When laypeople wanted to join the nuns, or monks, in praying the psalms, not knowing the Latin, they said instead the *Ave,* the 'Hail Mary' prayer, 150 times, one for each psalm. This later evolved into the familiar rosary practice.

ically, I've been getting spoiled by Eulalia. For those of you who don't know her, she's something else. Really something else.

EULALIA

THE LETTERS OF ANSELM TO EULALIA
TRANSLATED FROM THE LATIN BY GILLIAN KNIGHT

First letter, 1094 (Letter 361 in *Collected Letters*)

Anselm, by the disposition of God called Archbishop: to the lady and mother, the Reverend Abbess Eulalia and the holy congregation entrusted to her, to always advance in sanctity and attain to beatitude.

Although your holy zeal does not need admonition, the affection which I have towards you, and my office, compels me to write something to you in exhortation. Consider without ceasing, my most beloved daughters and Sisters, that you have undertaken and have already begun to ascend to Heaven, so that you may reign there and rejoice in reigning with your Lord and friend Jesus Christ, who expects you there and continually invites you in expectation. Indeed, as long as a man lives: he either ascends into Heaven by living well, or descends into Hell by living badly. If therefore you wish to attain to what you have proposed, it is necessary that you advance there by holy actions as if by certain steps. Therefore diligently examine the course of your life, not only in deeds but also in words; and not only in these but also in the slightest thoughts, lest by chance when you should in all these things always reach upwards, something be found there which is rather to go down. If you wish to guard well, it requires that you think of that which is most truly written: "who scorns the little things falls down little by little". For who falls down little by little does not advance but fails; and who fails, does not go up but goes down. Therefore take care anxiously for this, that you violate nothing, however small, which is of your order where God has placed you; and thus by holy steps to Heaven – may this happen with God's help! – you will ascend.

I pray that you may pray for me, and all the more attentively by how much you know that I trust in your affection; since never have I known myself to need your prayers more than now. For I am so badly in the archbishopric, that certainly – if I can speak without blame – I would prefer to depart from this life than to live thus.

Second Letter, 1104 (Letter 362)

Anselm Archbishop to his dearest sisters in Christ, Eulalia, Lady Abbess of Saint Edward and all her and his daughters, the greeting and blessing of God and of himself, as much as it is worth.

Your affection sought through a certain servant of the King, who brought me His seal, to be greeted, so he said, by a letter from me. I preferred to do this through my messenger, whom I knew I would soon be sending to England. I know that the abundance of true and pious affection makes you wish to see my letter gladly, so that since you cannot have my presence, which you desire with pious affection, according to your wishes you may at least show it to yourselves to some extent through my letter, and perhaps that you may stir up in me the memory of yourselves in case, so to speak, it fall asleep. I ascribe all of this to the magnitude of sincere affection. For I recognize that you truly remember me since you seek my letter that in it you may in some way behold me and rouse me to remember you. Just as I know that good will and sincerity of affection towards me does not grow cold in you, so you should know that in me it does not grow lukewarm towards you.

Most of all I wish you all to be mindful of me and to love me as you do by showing eagerness to be passionate without ceasing in the love of God, as you know my desire, and by striving, you who are subject to your Mother, to display obedience not to the eye but in the depths of the heart. I know that you are enduring adversity and tribulation from divers directions but then all the more must you be eager to set a guard to the Order and to your life, because you gain the consolation of God more by conducting your life well than if because of some worldly impediments you cease to any extent from the fervour of your undertaking.

In whatever secluded place you may be, be certain and have no doubt that each one has her angel, who sees and notes all her thoughts and acts and reports them to God the Judge. Therefore I advise you, dearest daughters, that in private and public each one of you should so guard all the movements of her heart and body as if she could see her guardian angel face to face with the eyes of the body. May Almighty God protect you with His blessing and bring you to the sight of His glory. Amen.

I know that you wish to know something of my return; but nothing certain can I write to you at present. Pray that it may happen according to the gracious will of God.

Third Letter, 1106 (Letter 363)

Anselm Archbishop: to the respected Abbess Eulalia and her daughters greetings.

I give thanks to your pious affection that you prayed for me, as long as I was in exile outside England, desiring my return; now I ask desirously that you pray that my return be fruitful. I wish you to know that my affection towards you since I have known you both lives and endures and by God's gift will endure as long as I live. Therefore although you do not need it since that same affection endures I will nevertheless write something to you so that you may know I love you and have concern for you.

I exhort and advise you, beloved Sisters and my daughters, to be subject and obedient to your Mother, not only to the human eye but also to the eye of God, for whom nothing is concealed. Then indeed it is true obedience when the will of the subject obeys the will of the one in charge, so that wherever the subject is he wishes what he understands the one in charge to wish, provided it is not contrary to the will of God. Your congregation must be a temple of God, and "the temple of God is holy". If therefore you live in a holy manner, as I hope, you are a temple of God. Indeed you live in a holy manner, if you keep carefully to your Order and undertaking. You do this diligently if you do not scorn the smallest things. Your undertaking must always strive to achievement and wholeheartedly dread failure. It is written: "Who despises small things gradually declines." Who declines does not succeed. Accordingly if you wish to succeed and dread to fail, do not despise the small things. Just as it is true: "Who despises small things gradually declines", so it is true that who does not despise small things gradually succeeds. Do not think that any sin is small, even though one is greater than another. For nothing which happens from disobedience – which alone cast out man from paradise – should be called small. For what sin will be small if, as the truth bears witness: "Who is angry with his brother will be judged guilty; and who says "Fool" (*racha*) will be found guilty by the council; and who says "Idiot" will be found guilty of the fires of Hell"? I ask, therefore, dearest daughters, that you neglect nothing, but always strive to guard your hearts as if in the sight of God.

Have peace amongst yourselves, because "In peace is made the place" of God, and "Much peace is to those who love the law of God", and "there is no stumbling block to them". I pray with heart and mouth for the blessing and absolution of God for you, and my own, for what it is worth, I give and entrust as much as I can. Farewell.

DEBORAH M JONES

ACKNOWLEDGMENTS

My thanks go to everyone who has helped and encouraged me with the research and production of this book, particularly to Dr Gillian Knight for her translations and insights into the Letters of St Anselm; my proofreader Barbara Hart; my beta-reader Janet Methley; the artist for the wonderful cover, Alison Merry; Janet Swiss for the sketches of Saxon buildings and the plan of the Abbey, and the book setter Danielle Wrate. Without these talented and generous people this little work could not have been realised.

ABOUT THE AUTHOR

Deborah M Jones is a retired theologian, editor and writer. Now, among many other activities, she works as librarian at Shaftesbury Abbey, Dorset, helping to create a research centre for studies on religious life between Saxon and Tudor times. This book, the second of a series of fictionalised accounts of certain abbesses at Shaftesbury Abbey, hopes to bring alive the women whose voices were not much heard, yet whose achievements were highly significant.

ALSO BY DEBORAH M JONES

Aethelgifu: First Saxon Abbess, The First Ladies of Shaftesbury Abbey, Vol I

Murder mysteries in the Julia Deane series:

The World according to Julia

Julia's World goes West

Julia's World in Tune

The Battles in Julia's World

(In preparation) Julia's World: All at Sea.

Nonfiction

The School of Compassion: a Roman Catholic theology of animals

For more information about Deborah and her books, visit www.deborahmjones.co.uk

Printed in Great Britain
by Amazon

40040131R00106